50 WAYS
TO LURE
YOUR
LOVER

Just wear a tight dress, Tess.
Put streaks in your hair, Claire.
Make the boy wait, Kate.
Polish your toes, Rose.
Show off some leg, Meg.
Bare your new tan, Ann.
Moan on the phone, Joan.
Dance until dawn, Fawn.
Give 'em a thrill, Jill.
Buy lingerie, Kay.
Get a tattoo, Sue.
Dangle your key, Dee.
Make love on a train, Jane.
Kiss and don't tell, Nell...

Turn the page and read all about it....

Dear Reader,

I have some very exciting news! In May of this year, we are launching a great new series called Harlequin Duets.

Harlequin Duets will offer two brand-new novels in one book for one low price. You will continue enjoying wonderful romantic comedy-type stories from more of the authors you've come to love! The two Harlequin Duets novels to be published every month will each contain two stories, creating four wonderful reading experiences each month. We're bringing you twice as much fun and romance with Harlequin Duets!

Longtime fan favorite Julie Kistler joins the Harlequin Love & Laughter line-up with *50 WAYS TO LURE YOUR LOVER*. Set in the offices of the fictional *Real Men* magazine (you'll find more of these stories in months to come), reporter Mabel Ivey finds herself the subject of a glamorous makeover and learns all about life as a sex object. She has to admit it's fun, but when the man of her dreams starts pursuing her, she's not sure if he's in love with the *new* her or the *real* her. Popular Temptation author Kate Hoffmann also makes her debut into the Love & Laughter series with *SWEET REVENGE?* The heroine, Tess Ryan, is in a bit of a fix. Her sister is hell-bent on getting revenge—on the man Tess has fallen in love with. Have fun watching revenge run amok in the most hilarious ways.

This is the last month you will find Love & Laughter on sale. I'd like to thank you for enjoying these stories—we, the editors, loved working on them. Don't forget to look for Harlequin Duets, on sale later this month!

Humorously yours,

Malle Vallik

Malle Vallik
Associate Senior Editor

50 WAYS
TO LURE
YOUR
LOVER

JULIE KISTLER

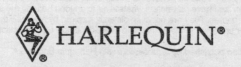

HARLEQUIN®

TORONTO • NEW YORK • LONDON
AMSTERDAM • PARIS • SYDNEY • HAMBURG
STOCKHOLM • ATHENS • TOKYO • MILAN • MADRID
PRAGUE • WARSAW • BUDAPEST • AUCKLAND

ISBN 0-373-44065-0

50 WAYS TO LURE YOUR LOVER

Printed in U.S.A.

A little about the author...

Julie Kistler loves combining screwball comedy with fantasy elements to come up with her own special mix of humor and romance. So, it was only a matter of time before Julie tried her hand at writing a book for Love & Laughter. And what an entrance she's made! Readers will delight in plain-Jane Mabel Ivey's transformation into a bombshell—with unexpected results. Fans might recognize Julie from Harlequin American Romance, where she's been a solid contributor to the line for the last ten years. Julie now lives in Illinois with her tall, dark and handsome husband and their cat, Thisbe.

To VLT, who took me to the L&L party;
to my boy Scott, who always knows how to
make me laugh; to my sister Nancy,
who shared stories of swing lessons;
and to the memory of my mom and the times
we stayed up late to watch Cary Grant in the
quintessential romantic comedies.

1

If you want to attract men without even trying, the first change you'll need to make is mental. Toss out all your outmoded ideas. Say, "No more Ms. Nice Girl!" Seize each and every day, each and every opportunity. Remember: when life hands you lemons, make lemonade. And when life hands you lemonade, drink up!

"SEIZE THE DAY," Mabel Ivey reminded herself.

Lifting her chin, squaring her shoulders and pasting on a confident smile, Mabel paused in front of the posh Loop offices of *Real Men* magazine, her hand on the fancy glass-and-chrome door.

She wasn't planning to stand there long—just long enough to take a deep breath before she went in. But she hadn't even had a chance to inhale, let alone exhale, before someone bashed into her from behind. Someone big and strong, decidedly male, someone in a whale of a hurry, someone who knocked her completely off-balance.

Balance was not her strong suit.

Mabel grabbed for the door to steady herself, but only managed to shove it open, her hand sliding along the chrome bar, unable to catch hold. And then she tripped, hurtling into the *Real Men* reception area, out of control, head over heels, making a kind of a hysterical "waaaah" sound as she fell. Her briefcase sailed away, flopping open in front of her, and one of her shoes flew off into space. As she hit the carpet, she felt her wire-rimmed glasses slip down her nose, dangling from one ear.

This was not the impression she'd hoped to make.

Scrambling to her knees, Mabel righted her glasses, grabbed for her shoe, and tried to shove a few pens and a hairbrush back into her briefcase. "What did you think you were doing?" she demanded, directing her words half over her shoulder at the human bulldozer. Then she muttered, "I guess it's par for the course. After my hair dryer blew up, my panty hose tanked, and I stuck mascara in my eye, I should've known someone like you would roll along."

"Sorry," he said dryly, offering a hand. "I've never seen anyone stop halfway through a door before. I was backing in, and I guess I ran into you."

She reached out to accept his help. But then she got a good look at him, and yanked back her hand as if he were a hot potato.

Oh, my God. He was gorgeous. Unbelievably gorgeous.

Her mind barely processed the details. Whoever he was—this undeniable force of nature—he was tall, broad-shouldered, and beautifully built. He wore a soft black T-shirt over black jeans, with a large bag of some sort slung over one shoulder. He had dark hair, a little rumpled, and thick, black lashes accenting eyes that were a singular color of deep, midnight blue. Those eyes were gazing right at Mabel. Words flooded her brain; words like *intense, stunning, mes-merizing....*

"Are you all right?" he asked.

All right? Mabel shook her head to clear his dev-astating impact. *She* looked like the wreck of the *Hes-perus,* while he looked like he'd just stepped out of the pages of *Real Men* magazine.

She stood, a little wobbly, but on her own, and reminded herself to breathe. If she got the job at *Real Men,* she would be around the sexiest, hottest men on the planet as a matter of course. So she'd better get used to it.

Every month, *Real Men* magazine answered Amer-ican women's fantasies with its bright, cheeky articles and saucy, seductive profiles. Glossy, fun, up-to-the-minute, it did its best to figure out what women wanted. And if the editors at *Real Men* were hiring this guy as a model, they were getting their money's worth. He looked a little older than the usual twenty-somethings, with their pink cheeks and boyish pouts, but he had whatever-it-was—sex appeal, sizzle, some-thing. He had *it.*

In fact, he had it all over the guys she'd seen on the pages of *Real Men.* Australia's Great Barrier Hunks. Bad Boys of Barbados. Hollywood He-Men. Chicago's Hottest Firefighters.

Mabel herself had contributed a short profile for that last one. Freelance, of course. Which didn't pay much. Which was why she needed a full-time job, like the one she was hoping and praying she'd get at *Real Men.* Which was why she shouldn't be hanging out at the front door, drooling over fantasy men like this one.

"Excuse me," she said with as much dignity as

she could muster, given the fact that she had just stumbled in the door and taken a header into the lobby. "I have a job interview in a few minutes."

"Maybe you should, uh…" he said kindly, waving a hand in the general direction of her face.

"What now?" Mabel was really starting to get cranky. Her hair was a mess because of the blow-dryer incident, she'd had to wear pants instead of her nice suit-skirt when her cat chewed on her panty hose, and *then* she'd had to abandon her contacts in favor of glasses after the thing with the mascara. If she were a less positive person, she might be thinking that the Fates were against her and this new job.

"What is it?" she asked again. "If you've got something to say, spit it out!"

"Nothing, nothing," Mr. Drop-Dead Gorgeous said quickly, backing off.

He clearly thought she was nuts.

"Well, it was all your fault," she grumbled. "You're the one who knocked me down."

But he was gone, whoever he was.

Once again, Mabel squared her shoulders, lifted her chin, and pasted on a smile. She headed toward the receptionist, but veered off at the last minute, worried by his reaction. So she slid into the rest room and tried to assess the damage.

"Uh-oh." Other than a big blob of misplaced makeup and a paper wad stuck in her hair, she didn't see anything wrong. What did the Bulldozer Boy think *he* saw?

"He saw plain old me. Apparently that was scary enough," she said out loud to the mirror.

Quickly, she brushed her hair and put on fresh lipstick, and then reported to the desk for her appointment. The receptionist barely looked up, simply directing her to another waiting area. As Mabel cleared the corner, she saw that this one was smaller and even plusher, and already occupied by—

"Oh, no," she said under her breath. "Him again!" She would have recognized those long, lean, black-jeans-encased legs anywhere. What was he doing here? Did he have an appointment with the senior editor, too? What for?

Mabel felt a moment of panic, but it quickly subsided. If he was a writer competing for the same job, Mabel was the Queen of Romania. She told herself he must certainly be a model—no one to fear.

At least he was buried behind a newspaper, so she didn't have to talk to him. Mabel took the chance to reorganize the papers in her briefcase, to take deep, calming breaths, and reestablish herself as a confident, poised woman before her interview.

"Is Mabel Ivey here?" a bored voice inquired.

Mabel looked up. The secretary—or perhaps she was an intern—couldn't have been more than twenty, and her skirt was cut so high she really shouldn't have bothered to wear one. She had a bone of some sort stuck through her broomstick-straight blond hair, frosted green lipstick, and legs that went on forever. Totally hip, totally cool. Mabel noticed that the newspaper across the room lowered far enough to take in the scandalous hemline.

Mabel shook her head at the folly of men. After all, the Bulldozer Boy was old enough to be the girl's...uncle.

"I'm Annika," the totally hip teen said with a twist of her lips that might have been a smile. "Ms. Weston's ready for you."

Mabel followed as the girl backed up into the inner sanctum. Once inside, Annika's voice dropped to a respectful hush. "Can I get you anything? Coffee? Latte?"

"No. No, thank you," Mabel replied, trying not to look at Annika's kicky little outfit and makeup. So young. So hip. But the girl and her miniskirt slipped out the door, no doubt to go back to the waiting room to flirt with the gorgeous man in black.

Mabel made an effort to forget him and the rest of her morning. Time to seize what was left of this day! She took a deep breath and tried to remain calm and poised as she stepped onto the pristine white carpet of the office, a few yards from Sophia Weston herself.

She'd met the senior features editor a few times before in the course of freelance assignments, and found her pleasant enough, easy to get along with, even if she was a different breed entirely. Tall, rail-thin, elegant to the bone, Sophia Weston was pretty intimidating to someone who didn't know a Manolo Blahnik pump from a plastic flip-flop.

"Mabel, so good to see you," the editor offered from behind her big-hunk-of-marble desk. Today she was wearing a bold tangerine suit in a fluid, expensive fabric. She gestured toward a chair. "I'm so glad you could come in. We have some exciting things happening here at *Real Men.*"

"I can't wait to hear all about it." One last time, Mabel wished in vain that the cat hadn't torn her panty hose and she hadn't stuck mascara in her eye. But it was too late now to lament her less-than-chic appearance. Taking one of the suede chairs that flanked the front of the mammoth desk, she crossed her legs carefully and folded her hands in her lap. She might not be flashy or fashionable, but she was presentable. Neat-and-tidy would have to do.

"If everything goes well," Sophia said, standing and leaning on the desk, "I think we might just have a spot for you here at *Real Men*. Full-time, on staff. What would you say to that?"

Mabel blinked. "I would say yes. Right now. I can start immediately."

"I appreciate your enthusiasm. That's what I was hoping to hear." The editor rose, circling around the desk, balancing herself artfully on its front edge. "But before we can get to a staff position, I have in mind a sort of trial assignment. Trial by fire, you might call it."

"Trial by fire?" Mabel echoed, her heart sinking. She'd never really been the fiery sort.

But Sophia Weston went right on, paying no attention to the doubtful tone. "Now you know," she confided, "I love your work. Love it. 'World Kisstory 101' was just terrific. And it doesn't get any better than 'Is Your Man a Poodle or a Tiger? Take the Animal Magnetism Test.'"

"Thank you. I liked that one myself," Mabel said modestly.

"A charming piece of writing. And it did very well with our focus groups." Sophia tilted back to gather a sheaf of papers from her desk, and then gazed more intently at her would-be employee. "But I'm going to need to see something more from you, Mabel, for you to make that leap from freelancer to full-time member of the *Real Men* team. What I'm going to need from you is more...well...intimacy. More heat."

"'Heat'? I—I'm not sure that's really me."

The editor nodded sagely. "Not yet. But we're taking the magazine in some bold new directions, and our staff has to be just as bold, just as hot. Let's face it, Mabel. While the stuff you've done for us so far has been funny and cute, it also hasn't really pushed any boundaries. So what I have in mind here is something a little different, something that will show us if you have what it takes for *Real Men*."

"And how would I show that?" Mabel inquired cautiously.

Sophia smiled, bending in a little closer. "It's really very easy. And great fun, too! I'm talking a chance of a lifetime, something any other woman would give her eyeteeth for—a *Real Men* makeover."

"Are you saying you want to give *me* a makeover?" That was a surprise. Okay, so she would have loved to be a glamour girl for about five minutes, just to impress the guys who didn't ask her to the prom, but a makeover? She was a writer, not a "before" picture in a magazine.

"I'm getting ahead of myself," Sophia said, waving a hand. "It's just that I'm so very enthusiastic about this project. All right, let's start at the beginning."

"Great." Mabel took a pen and a small pad out of her briefcase, ready to take notes.

"It's the fiftieth anniversary of *Real Men* this year," the editor continued, "and we're running a lot of special promotions, looking for features that will really launch us into our next fifty years with a bang. Our executive editor has come up with an interdepartmental project, a makeover piece, involving us here in Features, plus Beauty, Fashion, Fitness, even Food, where they'll do more in-depth work on the tips individually. Our working title for the whole project is '50 Ways to Lure Your Lover.' Fifty because of the fifty-year celebration, and luring a lover, because, well, isn't that every woman's fantasy, to attract men like flies to honey? Subhead: 50 Ways to Turn Yourself from Ho-Hum to Hot, from Sedate to Seductive. Don't you love it? You'd be involved in my part of the project, of course, here in Features. What do you think?''

"I'd love to work on something like that," Mabel said quickly, already guessing how she fit into the picture.

After all, she knew "ho-hum" from the inside out. And if it was writing they wanted, well, she could knock out some silly makeover article with both hands tied behind her back. Hadn't she sailed through "World Kisstory 101" when she hadn't been kissed since New Year's Eve 1995?

So they'd stick some poor schlemiel in a makeup chair, and Mabel would write a few paragraphs to go with the pictures. That didn't sound too tough.

Ms. Weston gave her a discriminating glance up and down, nodding her head as she went from stem to stern. "What I'm thinking is that we'll hire you to write the article, at your usual freelance terms. Plus, a hefty expense account to cover this particular assignment. And if it turns out as terrific as I know you can make it, why, I'll put you on staff. That's a promise.''

Mabel tried not to get too hopeful, even though the talk of a hefty expense account was almost enough to have her doing cartwheels, all by itself. Still, she knew this was no done deal. *"As terrific as I know you can make it..."* Sophia Weston was going to be judging that article as critically as she was right now eyeing the line of Mabel's boring black pants and the ordinary cut of her brown hair.

But whether the writing assignment was going to be a breeze or an ordeal, it didn't matter. Deep in her heart, Mabel knew she had no choice. Her current patchwork of writing assignments barely paid the rent on her terrible apartment, she was living on rice and beans, and her cat was an illegal alien because she couldn't afford the city registration fee. She needed this job, come hell or high water, come makeover or Mayday.

"So what I'm looking for," the editor continued, "is a feature piece with a spunky, irreverent tone. This should be sort of an undercover odyssey to illustrate these—" she scanned the paper in her hand "'—Fifty Nifty Makeover Ideas for Every Plain Jane Who's Ever Yearned to Walk on the Wild Side.'"

"Did you say 'undercover odyssey'?" What the heck did that mean?

"That's what makes it so fascinating," Sophia enthused. "We start with a Plain Jane, but not just any old Plain Jane—we need one who can write. So you can see why I thought of you. I can honestly say, you're perfect for it!"

Plain Jane. *Oh, dear.* They wanted her *because* she was wearing ugly pants and glasses, *because* she had no clue how to arrange her bangs for maximum sex appeal, *because* she'd never in her life seduced a man by candlelight while wearing nothing but edible flowers. Someone who was already the total *Real Men* package wouldn't do. No, it had to be someone who was definitely not cool or hip or sexy. Someone like Mabel.

Sophia gave her an encouraging smile. "Normally, for a makeover, we'd just pull the subject into the studio and set the experts on her. But this time, we want it to be just as if she were a reader at home, seeing these ideas and reacting spontaneously, with no help from us. So our Plain Jane—that would be you—tries out some of the fifty suggestions, records her thoughts and observations, struts her newly *hot* stuff in front of some likely contenders, and tells the readers of *Real Men* all about it. You get to walk on the wild side, Mabel. Won't that be fun?"

Putting aside for the moment that Sophia considered her a perfect Plain Jane, which was demoralizing enough, Mabel would certainly never have admitted to any hankering to walk on any wild side! Fun? "The wild side" sounded pretty scary to her. Like getting stuck inside the lion's cage while wearing Raw Meat perfume.

But a small voice reminded her just how much she needed this job.

"The tips are all wonderful. You're going to love them," Ms. Weston assured her. "We've done them to kind of parody the lyrics of the Paul Simon song. You know, "Fifty Ways to Leave Your Lover"? Of course, this is the opposite, since this is about *luring* one, not *leaving* one. But there's real substance here, too. That's what's so great! Like number one, 'Jump at the chance, Nance.' You see, it's all about empowerment, more than makeup or clothes. Although those things are certainly included—you know, sexy shoes, undies, hair color, fingernails, cleavage, even tattoos and body piercing—the works."

Mabel's mind was whirling. Cleavage was bad enough, but tattoos? Body piercing? "I've never really liked being in the spotlight," she admitted finally. "And some of these things... Well, they're just not me."

"But you'll almost be in disguise," Sophia tried. "You'll be a whole new you. And the fact that you're reticent about it is exactly what we need. You have a unique perspective."

"I guess, in a way... I mean, I *am* different," Mabel allowed, thinking about Annika, the girl with the iridescent green lips and nonexistent skirt. If that was "normal" for *Real Men*, then Mabel was anything but.

"Maybe other Plain Janes out there would like to see that the wildlife, and wild men, can be tamed," Sophia said shrewdly. "And aren't you just the woman to do it?"

Mabel didn't say anything to the editor, but she had to admit, she was getting this small, funny feeling deep inside her....

She thought about the way that hunk in the lobby had lowered his newspaper to catch Annika's frisky hemline. No one ever did that to *her*.

If she followed the magazine's advice to heat up her image, would men, well, *pant* after her? What would it be like to stride into a bar or a party, and have every man there want her?

She couldn't help wondering if being a femme fatale for the first time in her life, leading a couple of unsuspecting guys around by the nose, might not be sort of fun.

Was it possible? Did Sophia Weston see some budding beauty, a hidden vixen, behind Mabel's wire-rims?

"Okay," she said suddenly. "I'll do it."

"Fabulous." Sophia Weston beamed at her. "Take a deep breath, sweetie, because you're not going to believe my next piece of news. It's even more exciting!"

Mabel was still getting used to the idea of getting in touch with her "inner vixen," so she wasn't quite ready to move on to any more excitement just yet. "What could be better than cleavage and tattoos and body piercing?" she asked weakly.

"I'm talking the stuff of dreams here, m'dear," the editor offered, bending over closer and dropping her voice as if they were co-conspirators in some mad scheme. Well, in a way they were. "I have just two words for you." She pounced. "Trace Cameron."

"The guy who did all those swimsuit editions?" Mabel had heard the name, of course, although she'd never seen his face. He was a famous photographer. Or maybe *infamous* was a better word.

"He practically reinvented swimsuit editions," Sophia crowed. "And then there were his fashion shoots for *Vogue* and *Elle,* not to mention the amazing celebrity portraits for the cover of *Vanity Fair.* He's the crème de la crème. Snowdon? Herb Ritts? Annie Leibowitz? Trace Cameron puts them all to shame."

"Didn't he...?" She didn't know quite how to put it. "*NY* magazine, wasn't it?"

"He put *NY* on the map," the editor noted. "You don't get any better, any hotter than that. He created the whole *NY* visual style. Wow!" There was a gleam in her eye. "And we've got him. Well, what can I say? *NY*'s loss is our gain."

Mable noticed her would-be boss wasn't talking about exactly why *NY* had "lost" Mr. Cameron. She didn't have to. Everyone in the magazine world with access to E-mail or a telephone had already heard the gossip.

It was absolutely true that he'd been hotter than a pistol in the world of fashion photography during his tenure at *NY*. He was known for sizzle and edge in his work, for making two-dimensional supermodels actually look like there was a *there* there. Mabel didn't know quite what it was—she only bought the magazines for market research and usually skipped the photos—but he certainly had made a name for himself.

A large part of that name, however, stemmed from his tempestuous, very public relationship with flamboyant Rita Devon, executive editor of *NY*. As a team, they'd sent the magazine to the top of the charts. According to the gossip, they'd also danced the night away in London discos, thrown several plates of seafood and a few bottles of wine at each other during a shouting match in Milan, kissed and made up in Paris, then split for good, back in New York.

After which Rita had dumped him from the *NY* masthead. Ouch. No girlfriend, no job. People loved his photos, but the thing with Rita had made him just a bit, well, suspect. Was it his talent for photography that had gotten him ahead, or a knack for romancing his lady bosses?

"So he'll be working for *Real Men* now?" Mabel inquired.

"Oh, yes. This is such a coup for us," Sophia confided, excitement threading her words. "Well! You can imagine."

"Uh, oh, sure. Definitely. Congratulations." Mabel spent a second or two wondering whether the elegant Ms. Weston was the boss du jour in Trace Cameron's life. Surely not. Sophia was so together, so perfect. What would she want with another editor's leftovers? Mabel imagined him as an aging, boozing, jet-setting Lothario, his face lined and haggard from too much carousing with supermodels and The Rolling Stones. Would Sophia go for someone like that? It didn't seem likely. But you never knew.

"Congratulations to you, too, sweetie. I'm sure you're thrilled to hear you'll be working so closely with Trace," Ms. Weston said breathlessly.

"Me? Working with him?" Mabel blinked. And then she gasped. "Oh, I get it. You're going to have him take my 'after' photos, to make them really glamorous."

Just think, the same guy who'd spent years making Cindy Crawford and Naomi Campbell look even more beautiful than they already were would be photographing regular old girl-off-the-street Mabel Ivey. *Good heavens!*

"Not just your 'after,'" Ms. Weston announced happily. "His first assignment for *Real Men* is to photograph every little detail of your transformation!"

"'E-every little detail'?" Mabel gulped. Not only was she in doubt about whether she wanted to transform, she sure didn't want to do it in front of the likes of Trace Cameron! Why, the man probably hadn't seen a normal woman in years. All he knew were slashing cheekbones, luscious bosoms heaving out of tiny bikini tops, impossibly long legs and even more impossibly thin thighs. Mabel felt the stirrings of panic. "When you say 'every little detail,' exactly how much detail do you mean?"

Sophia shrugged. "The two of you will hash out

what pictures you think best suit the story. And, of course, what story best suits the pictures.''

"Well, he's not going to be following me around or anything, is he? I mean, he can take a few photos of me in a makeup chair, all plain and untouched, and then a few more after I try the tips.'' Mabel was trying to be optimistic about this. Or at least professional. But she really didn't like the idea of dancing to some prima donna photographer's tune when a real job hung in the balance. "I'm sure he'll be much too busy imprinting his new visual style on the rest of the magazine to fool with me. Right?''

"Oh, no, no, no!'' Ms. Weston rose and slipped back behind her desk, looking impatient. "You and this article will be his only focus, to start out. Remember, we're talking about *Real Men*, here. Our fiftieth anniversary! We need excitement. Intimacy! Heat!''

'Heat'? Not that again!

"You and Trace are in this together,'' Sophia stressed. "I have to see your words and his pictures leap off the page. Vivid, vital, in the moment. Not just okay. Not just good enough. Fabulous! Hotter than a steam furnace on the Fourth of July!'' She frowned, crossing her arms over her striking tangerine suit. "No heat, no job.''

Mabel stiffened her spine. Okay, so she would invent a new concept of "heat.''

So what if this celebrity photo jock was likely to run screaming from the room the first time he saw her? Or even worse—run *laughing* from the room?

She would get along with him. She would do what she had to do. She would find the excitement *Real*

Men and Sophia Weston were looking for. She would get this job!

She pictured it in her mind: full-time, on staff, with an office and a byline. Maybe even a window and a potted plant. With a steady salary, she could afford a decent apartment, as many cans of Fancy Feast as Polly could hold, a new winter coat....

No matter how many photographic devils she had to dance with, she would get this job.

"Where do I start?" she asked, sitting up straight and meeting Sophia Weston's gaze.

"First, let's get the man himself in here to meet you." The editor pressed a button on her phone. "Annika, could you bring in Mr. Cameron, please? Thanks, sweetie."

"He's here? Now?" She'd hoped to have a minute to change her clothes, spruce up a bit, before she had to meet him. Time for some research might have been nice, so she could figure out why people thought his photos were special, or who he was under the slick shutterbug facade. She would have loved time to plot out a strategy for getting along with the guy.

But there was no chance for any of that. She was just considering whether to try to hide her glasses in her pocket when the door to the office opened.

And *he* walked in.

She'd never seen a photo of Trace Cameron, but somehow, she had been expecting a preening, graying, middle-aged man with a ponytail and an earring, a drink in one hand and a cigarette in the other, someone who had assistants scurrying this way and that, bringing lenses and lights and equipment whenever he snapped his fingers.

Not this guy. He was all by himself.

He didn't need anybody else.

He was gorgeous—as good-looking as any model he'd ever shot. One swift glance was all it took to do an inventory. Tall, broad-shouldered, about thirty, beautifully if casually dressed in a soft, dark T-shirt and black jeans, carelessly toting a leather camera bag over one shoulder.

It wasn't so much his features, although they looked great from here, or even his body, which was lean and fit, with everything exactly where it should have been.

No, it was in the way he held himself—relaxed and unstudied, a little arrogant, a *lot* sexy.

Mabel closed her eyes. She should have known.

Bulldozer Boy.

2

Tip #32: Strike a hot pose, Rose.

Is there a man alive who wouldn't like to see sexy, alluring photos of his lady? Glam photos are easy to get, not expensive, and will remind him of your smoldering eyes long after you've left the bedroom. How hot those poses are is up to you, of course!

"I DIDN'T EXPECT TO SEE you again so soon," he said. Was that a spark of mischief in his deep blue eyes? Or just the reflection from Sophia Weston's recessed lighting?

Mabel tried to get her lips to move, but she had become paralyzed as soon as he walked into the room. Of all the terrible luck! She was assigned to work day and night with the most magnificent man in the history of the universe, and she'd already bashed into him, fallen into a lump at his feet, yelled at him, and proved to him that she was a graceless, uncoordinated dim bulb who scattered glasses and shoes and briefcases wherever she went.

"Oh, so you two have already met?" Ms. Weston asked eagerly.

"We ran into each other as we came into the build-

ing,'' Trace Cameron responded dryly. "I'm happy
to see you again, Ms. Ivey. Or should I call you Mabel?"

"M-Mabel is fine."

She wanted to sink under the snowy-white carpet.
But then he turned that beautiful gaze back to her,
regarding her thoughtfully, making her feel like she
was a marshmallow toasting on an open fire. Could
she help it if she was warming up a little?

"When I saw you come into the waiting room, it
occurred to me it might be you," he mused. "You fit
Sophia's description pretty well."

Sure, she did. Plain Jane, right? Probably the only
one running around *Real Men. So snap out of it!* she
commanded herself. When you were a Plain Jane, you
couldn't afford to get all gooey every time someone
like Bulldozer Boy so much as glanced at you. She
was going to have to work with this man. And drooling all over him was not the way to do it.

"So you've both signed on to the project," Sophia
announced, draping a hand over Mabel's shoulder,
nudging her closer to Trace. "I know you're going to
have such fun together. I should warn you, though,
Mr. Cameron has quite the reputation."

For romancing his bosses? Surprised that Ms. Weston would bring up his *NY* debacle so carelessly, Mabel stuttered, "Oh, well, you know— I mean, I *had*
heard something...."

His dark brows lowered ominously, but Sophia slid
right on without a pause. She declared, "They say all
the women he photographs fall madly in love with
him. So you'd better watch out, Mabel, sweetie!"

"I don't think that will be a problem," the two of

them announced in unison. And then they looked at each other, each one a little taken aback.

Aloud, he explained, with a slight edge in his voice, "I can't speak for Ms. Ivey, of course, but it's not going to be a problem for me. After my last job…" He winced. "After that experience, I made a vow. No mixing business with pleasure. Ever. Thanks for mentioning it, Sophia. I'm glad to get that out of the way right off the bat."

"Me, too," Mabel agreed quickly. "I mean, that's a really good rule, and I'm sure it's very smart to just, you know, say it right up front. Especially considering the nature of the, uh, assignment, what with walking on the wild side and all. I mean, it's a great idea to set the, uh, ground rules and all."

She wondered if she sounded as silly as she felt. As if anyone in this room thought that *he* would worry about mixing business with pleasure with *her*. Clearly this warning was meant to nip in the bud any crazy crushes Mabel might form. That was fine with her.

She lifted her chin. "I'm not in the market."

"Me, either."

"Good."

"Great."

"Perfect." She extended a hand and offered a tight smile. "I think we'll do just fine together."

His lips curved into a charming grin. "So do I." He took her hand, and she had to grit her teeth and hang on, not to melt into a puddle right there. Talk about electricity. How did he do that? *Snap out of it,* she told herself again, more heatedly this time.

"So, Mabel," he went on, "I think I'm clear on what the assignment is."

"Make a silk purse out of me?" she asked lightly, trying not to feel wounded by the whole thing. "You're the expert. What do you think? Have we got a chance of pulling this off?"

His grin widened, and it was practically diabolical. "No sweat. The only hard part will be convincing anyone you were ever a 'before.'"

Oh, heavens. He was gallant, too. Mabel felt a little flushed.

"I'm pleased you two seem to be getting along so well, since after all, this *is* a team effort. The words and the pictures have to work intimately together, which means the two of you will, too." Sophia paged through a stack of documents. "Let's see... We've got the authorization for your expense accounts here, advance checks to get you started, the list of tips you'll be following—you know, the actual 'Fifty Ways to Lure Your Lover,' some suggestions of places you might want to try to pick up clothes and accessories, and a copy of the schedule, for when we need what." She gave them both an expectant smile as she handed over the folders. "So, kids, it's up to you. Go for it, have fun, and make magic!"

Mabel took a deep breath. When she'd decided to seize the day, she hadn't exactly had this much seizing in mind. Working intimately with Trace Cameron? Her mind boggled.

"Mabel?" Trace asked softly.

She blinked. "Uh-huh?"

"Are you ready?"

"As ready as I'm ever going to be."

"Let's do it," he said.

Trace Cameron led the way out of the office, and Mabel followed, her eyes on the sleek, dark hair that just reached his collar. She didn't dare look any lower.

Why did she get the feeling her life was never going to be the same again?

MABEL CURLED UP ON the sofa. "Polly," she called, trying to entice her cat to sit on her lap and purr like a good kitty should. Petting an animal was supposed to bring your blood pressure down—Mabel had written about it in a "stress-busters" article she'd done for the *Super Seniors* newsletter—and at the moment, she needed all the help she could get. "Polly? Come here, baby."

Polly ignored her. She was occupied, licking a paw, swatting at invisible insects, carrying on an independent life.

"Yeah, sure, I need you and you're too busy."

The cat flipped her tail and sauntered off, clearly not in the mood to comfort her "human."

"This whole thing is all your fault!" Mabel called after her. "I'm only taking the job to make you legal, you know."

No response. Except for the dubious sound of bashing and crashing in the bedroom closet.

Mabel let out a quick cry of frustration and dropped her head back onto the arm of the couch. Safe at home, wearing her favorite cotton pajama bottoms and a loose White Sox T-shirt, she should have been comfortable and relaxed. Instead, her case of rampant anxiety was getting worse.

"What is wrong with me?"

She'd been sitting here stewing for two hours, and all she had to show for it was a blank legal pad. She had to figure this out pronto, to come up with a logical schedule of how this article was going to be accomplished. Because if she didn't, she'd never make it wonderful enough to impress Sophia Weston into giving her that job.

And Trace Cameron would be bulldozing her into *his* way before she had a chance to open her mouth.

"Why did I say I would do this?"

She jumped up, grabbed the folder from *Real Men* off the table, and flipped it open one more time. It hadn't gotten any better since the last time she'd looked at it.

"Oh, good heavens," she moaned, glancing at random items on the list. "If I follow these tips, I'll look like Bozo the Clown! 'Stock up on henna, Jenna. All it takes is a quick rinse to launch the Attack of the Killer Redhead.' Me? A redhead? Or this one. 'Sharpen your claws, Roz.' That doesn't even rhyme." She read on, "'One look at your untamed fingernails, and he'll be unable to think of anything but the tracks you'll leave on his back.'"

She paused, chewing the end of her pen. She didn't really get that. Why would a man fantasize about bodily harm? After all, getting scratched by some woman's long nails wasn't a *fun* thing.

It took her a second. Someone raking someone's back, like in the throes of… "Eeuuwwww." That was kind of gross, wasn't it? She gave her own short, neatly filed nails a jaded look. "As if."

Shaking her head, Mabel continued down the inventory of fifty nifty ideas. "So if I don't like those I can get a peekaboo tattoo to make him want to uncover my other secrets, or create incredible cleavage with gel breast-packs and a Wonderbra."

This time she hazarded a peek at her unremarkable

chest, even more unremarkable under the baggy T-shirt. No gel inserts or push-up bras had a hope of turning her into Chesty LaRue. "I'm dead. That's all there is to it. I'm dead."

And the list didn't get any better after that. If more bounteous bosoms weren't her style, she sure didn't see herself in a skirt cut up to here, like it told her to do under Tip #8, titled "Show off some leg, Meg," or the see-through black lace advocated by Tip #31, "Give 'em a thrill, Jill."

Okay, so it was kind of…titillating, in a weird sort of way. But that wasn't Mabel's way! In her normal life, she wouldn't even want to think about this stuff, let alone figure out how to turn it into a story.

Still, if she were honest with herself, the makeover ideas weren't the really scary part. Not by a long shot. What really made her break out in hives was that she was going to have to share the whole experience with *him.*

"How can I possibly even discuss these things with him?" she wailed, envisioning the conversation. "So, Trace, next Tuesday we can look for black garter belts or animal-print thongs. Which do you prefer?"

As if on cue, her doorbell rang.

Mabel just sat there for a second. Some sixth sense had already told her who it was, but she figured if she didn't answer, maybe he would go away.

Not Bulldozer Boy. Going away wasn't his style.

"Mabel, open up," he called, knocking loudly as he spoke. "I know you're in there."

She stormed over and yanked open the door. He'd thrown a leather jacket over a sweater and jeans, but otherwise he looked just as amazing as he had before.

Drop-dead gorgeous, in other words. She steeled herself. "What are you doing here?"

"When I put you into a taxi on Michigan Avenue, we agreed to get together later to get started," he reminded her.

"Well, yes, I know, but when I said 'later' I didn't mean *now*. I meant later."

He paused. "This is later."

"Not that much later."

"Later enough." Easing his ever-present camera bag in first, he slid past her into the apartment, leaving Mabel hanging in the doorway. "Cute place."

"I like it," she said, trying not to sound defensive.

She knew very well that her apartment was small and cramped, always either too cold or too hot, and the plumbing made awful screeching noises late at night. But it was also bright and fairly cheerful, with a nice window for Polly to sit in. And very cheap, which was the main thing. She didn't expect someone like the mighty Trace Cameron, jet-setter, to appreciate a one-bedroom apartment with a view of the Knights of Columbus parking lot. But she actually did like it.

Trace was already inside, poking his head around corners, perusing her eccentric attempts at decoration, scanning her wacky refrigerator-magnet collection, generally making himself at home.

Mabel frowned, belatedly shutting the front door. "Okay, so even if this is later enough to be later, why did you come here? We didn't say we'd meet *here*," she noted.

He shrugged. "It just seemed like the best way to cut to the chase."

It really annoyed her that he was skipping ahead,

not following the proper steps. He was supposed to call, they'd have a polite chat, they'd check their respective schedules, they'd set up a meeting at some neutral location.... Not *this*. Not *now*. "How could you know I'd be here?"

He grinned, cutting right in. "I figured the odds were about three-to-one you were home, going over the materials for the article." He inclined his head to indicate the open folder on the coffee table. "Looks like I'm on the money on that one."

"But I could've been out, picking up..." She was determined to think of something to dent his infuriating attitude, some reason she should not have been home. "I could've needed to go to the bank. Or had to go out to walk my dog."

He sent her a sardonic glance, slipping the bag and the jacket off his shoulders as he dropped lazily to the sofa. "You hit the bank on your way back from *Real Men,* so you could deposit the advance check first thing. And you have a cat, not a dog."

The deposit slip was sitting on the coffee table, and her cat's bowl, the one that said Tuna Breath on it, was in plain sight over by the alcove she called a kitchen. She had to hand it to him; he was observant, if irritating.

"Well, I still could've been gone," she said stiffly. "You couldn't know."

He just smiled up at her, stretching out his long legs. "I play the odds. It works for me."

"Uh-huh." Mabel sort of hovered there, unsure what to do next. This was a new feeling for her. She was usually so good at making lists, plotting a logical, linear path from point A to point B. But he kept getting her off track!

"Mabel, are you ready to get started?"

"Right." Distracted, she tried to decide where to sit. It was a choice of a wobbly rocking chair, the hardwood floor, or the couch. Next to him? No way. She took the rocker, balancing herself gingerly on the front edge.

He was staring down into her folder, right at that blasted list, right at the garter belts and breast packs and animal-print thong. Even the words—in plain black-and-white on the page—made her feel hot and dizzy.

"So," she began awkwardly, feeling her cheeks begin to flame, "if we're going to plan this out, I thought maybe I should, you know, look over the, uh, list, and, kind of, um, pick a few. Then we can figure out how best to, you know, illustrate this makeover thing. How does that sound?"

"Wouldn't want to plan ahead too far," he returned. "Takes all the spark out of it."

"You don't want to plan ahead?" Not even a little plan? If she hadn't already been panicking, that would have sent her over the edge.

He didn't answer. He seemed to be busy giving her apartment the once-over, casting a critical eye this way and that. "I'd love to do it in front of the refrigerator. The magnets are fun—especially the local souvenirs and The Brady Bunch. I always thought Jan was cuter than Marcia, didn't you?"

"What are you talking about? Do what in front of the refrigerator?"

But he had already moved back into the living room. "The light's better in here. Maybe over by the window," he said thoughtfully.

Rising, he strode over there, hauling his camera bag

with him, pulling out a couple of cameras, a light meter and a folded tripod as he went. While Mabel watched, mystified, he pushed aside the lace curtain at her window, rearranged the tendrils of her hanging spider plant, and dragged a stool over from her breakfast bar.

"Where's the cat?" he asked, screwing a camera into the tripod. "That might be a nice touch."

"What are you doing?" Mabel demanded. She had never been the hand-wringing, foot-stamping sort, but she almost wished she were.

"Oh. I thought it was obvious." He indicated the stool. "Come sit here. We're doing the 'before' shots. You know, the 'ho-hum,' before you get 'hot.'"

"Now? Here? But, but—"

"Might as well get started. It'll just take a minute." His gaze held hers expectantly. "Don't worry. This is supposed to be your regular old look—plain, unvarnished you." When she didn't move, he offered a small smile. "Repeat after me: Spontaneity is good."

"I don't think so."

He tilted his head slightly to one side, narrowing his eyes. "Definitely keep the shirt. It's just exactly what we need for this shot."

Her old gray White Sox jersey? "You're going to take my picture in *this?*"

"It's perfect. It tells a story all by itself," he told her. "The gray is good—kind of washed-out and dull on film—plus it establishes the location. I mean, you pretty much have to be in Chicago to be a White Sox fan. And it says humdrum, like you haven't got much of a social life."

"I think even women with dates sometimes wear team T-shirts," she said indignantly.

"Well, maybe." He focused on her shirt, and she immediately crossed her arms over her chest, wishing she hadn't brought it up, wishing she'd worn a bra. "Looks good to me."

She didn't know whether he meant the shirt and its dubious distinction as a "before" subject, or the woman underneath. Either way, she didn't like his scrutiny.

His gaze flickered up to meet hers. "What about the cat?"

"The cat? What about the cat?"

"Just a general rule, people warm up and take better pictures if they're holding babies or pets." He sent a quick look around the floor. "So where's the cat?"

"I think she's in the bedroom, but she isn't exactly, well, cooperative."

He lifted one dark brow. "Cats aren't supposed to be cooperative. But don't worry—they like me."

So now he was a pet expert, too. Mabel backed away into the bedroom, in search of her dear little kitty. As she yanked Polly out from under the bed, the cat growled ominously. Mabel smiled. Polly hated everyone except Mabel, and she wasn't even too thrilled with her roommate right at the moment. The bad-tempered tabby could be counted on to take a whack at Trace, or pounce on his foot and scratch the leather of his expensive shoe. And wouldn't that be fun?

Polly squirmed and caterwauled the few steps back into the main part of the apartment, making an attack seem promising. But when Trace walked right up beside them, the cat surprised her by sniffing his outstretched fingers delicately. Still, Mabel braced herself for the inevitable hissing and spitting.

But no. Polly bumped her head against his hand and began to purr so loudly the neighbors could probably hear it.

"Here, I'll take her," he offered, scooping the mysteriously limp and compliant cat right out of Mabel's arms. He turned her upside down and cooed at her.

What was this all about? Mabel was stunned. Polly had allowed herself to be approached and now *held* by a stranger. It was as if her snarly tabby had been replaced by a Stepford cat. Maybe Prozac had been hidden in her Little Friskies.

Or maybe Trace Cameron's way with females extended to the animal kingdom.

Mabel was so shocked, she didn't even fuss when he led her to the stool and positioned her just so, and then handed over her cat. He stepped back immediately and began clicking away, as she tipped her head down to give Polly a talking-to for her behavior.

After a moment, Trace stopped abruptly. "This isn't working."

"Oh, I'm sorry. Is it the way I'm sitting?" Mabel knew she was no model, but she'd thought she was doing okay. "If this looks, you know, stiff or something, I can move."

"No, that's not the problem." He frowned, contemplating the scene. "You look too good. With the cat on your lap and the light from the window glowing on the top of your head... Great stuff. I could sell it in a minute as an ad for tea cozies. But not as a 'before' picture."

"Oh." Mabel smiled. It was the best news she'd had in a long time.

"Weren't you wearing glasses at Sophia's office? We need those. And drop the cat."

When she did as commanded, the little traitor ran right over and rubbed her head against Trace's pant leg. But he was too caught up in his new idea to do more than absently stoop and scratch her ears.

"Mabel, I changed my mind about the glasses. Lose them, okay? Let's try you in the rocker. Don't smile, try to keep your mind blank, and just stare me right in the eye, okay?"

Following his instructions, Mabel was a little uncomfortable, especially since he was closer now—not at the tripod, but holding his camera in his hands. He kept veering in and out, leaning over her in the rocker, reaching out to tip her chin up a fraction, to tuck her hair behind her ear for a few shots, then back to rearrange her bangs. She tried to sink back into the cushions as much as she could, but even when he was several feet away, with a camera between them, she could still feel the imprint of his fingers and the moody sweep of his gaze.

"Is this better? Am I ugly enough now?" she asked darkly.

"Naaaaw." His tone was wry as he cupped her face and tilted it to one side. "You've got this waif thing going that could give Kate Moss a run for her money."

"'Waif'? I don't think so." *You should see my thighs,* she thought, but she kept it to herself. As he fooled with just how he wanted her to hold her face, he braced a knee on the chair next to her hip, and he seemed very warm and very near. Suddenly her brain was having trouble forming thoughts other than *I*

*could wrap my arms around him in two seconds flat
and pull him down into this rocker with me....*

"So, Mabel, talk to me," Trace said, interrupting
her reverie. "What are you thinking about?"

"Uh, nothing," she said quickly. "Why?"

"Because your eyes got all wide and soft, and there
was definitely something going on there that didn't fit
this   poor-girl-who-can't-get-a-date   profile." He
stood, releasing her. "So whatever it was you were
thinking about, don't think it again, okay?"

"No problem. It's gone." She hoped she wasn't
blushing.

"Stand over here, by this wall. I've got a new
idea."

Abrupt one minute, mocking the next, and then
reading her mind... He really was unlike anyone
she'd ever known, and it had nothing to do with his
looks. Well, okay, part of it was probably his looks.
How often did you run across a man who put Mel
Gibson to shame? But the rest of it was inside him—
that bulldozer quality, the confidence and arrogance
and charm that made it easy to understand why every
woman he photographed supposedly fell in love with
him.

Right now, she was finding him absolutely fascinating.

"Mabel, you've got that look again. Try hating my
guts instead. Give me the expression you gave me
when I knocked you down at *Real Men.*"

"I didn't hate your guts," she said softly. "I was
miffed for a second, but that was it."

"Okay, so pretend."

She did her best to glare. "I'm kind of awkward

at this, you know, this pretending to be something I'm not."

He kept clicking the shutter, although she had no idea whether any of this was usable. Why was he taking so many pictures? "That's all right," he murmured. "Awkward is good."

"I don't think so."

"Don't look at me. Think cranky." He paused, running an impatient hand through his hair. "I know," he said, taking her arm and pulling her over by the sofa. "Lie down here on the floor, flat on your back. Just look up at the ceiling, not at me. Think about Sophia's list—those fifty ways to turn yourself into a siren. That made you cranky, didn't it? All that hot stuff. Tell me, which one did you like the least?"

She stretched out on the hardwood, feeling like a lump of clay as Trace moved to arrange her the way he wanted her. He fiddled with her hair, fanning it out around her head, and then nudged her arms straight down next to her body.

"Is this absolutely necessary?" she asked, not appreciating being laid out like Snow White after having eaten the poisoned apple. "Don't you have enough pictures already?"

"Who's the expert here?"

She didn't bother to answer. But reclining flat on her back with him hovering above her was giving her ideas again—ideas she didn't want. She tried to think unpleasant thoughts. But there he was, his long legs just in her periphery, his clever hands balancing the camera, his midnight-blue eyes running up and down her every which way.

"So," he tried again, "which one of the fifty tips annoys you the most?"

She chewed her lip. No way was she coming out with specifics. Besides, how could you choose from among G-strings and corsets, rings in your navel and tattoos on your butt? Or any of the rest of them, for that matter? She declared, "I don't have a problem with any of them."

He let the camera drop, but bent nearer, his face right over hers. "You're lying to me, Mabel. It's driving you nuts. All that slinky lingerie and spike heels and chocolate shaped like body parts."

"There's no chocolate shaped like body parts on the list!" she protested, as his lens zeroed in once more.

"No? I must've misread it."

"And it is not driving me nuts." He'd told her not to look at him, but she did anyway, wishing he weren't quite so unsettling. "They're just for fun, you know, with the rhymes and everything. I thought 'Jump at the chance, Nance' was very empowering."

"'Empowering,' huh?" She couldn't see his smile, but she could hear it in his voice.

He zoomed in closer—much too close for comfort. Mabel's whole body felt itchy and twitchy with him there, above her, around her, just out of reach.

"How about if we make one up just for you?" he teased, crouching next to her, bending to whisper in her ear. "Let's see. What can I think of?"

She held her breath. What was he doing? She could smell him, sense his body heat, feel the warm puff of his soft words on her cheek. If she hadn't been lying down, she would have fallen there.

"I've got it." His voice dropped into a huskier register when he murmured, "Get naked in sable, Mabel."

"'N-naked in sable'?" She thought she might die right there. Whether she was getting a full body blush or starting to ignite, she couldn't say.

Click, click.

"That's the one I wanted," he said with satisfaction. And then he sat back on his heels and laughed out loud. "Wow. That was good."

Mabel scrambled to sit up. What had just happened here? "You couldn't possibly want that for the Plain Jane picture! That wasn't right at all!"

"Nope. That one's for me." And then he winked at her.

3

Tip #13: Wear a tight dress, Tess.

Try a long, slinky tank dress in a clingy fabric—
and nothing but you underneath! Or a curve-
conscious minidress in an eye-popping knit.

The possibilities are endless. If you've got the
body, show it off! And if you don't, see Tip
#41: Get to the gym, Kim.

JUMPING TO HER FEET, Mabel didn't know whether to
hit him or kiss him. After all, it was kind of a compliment, that he would want a picture of her not for
the magazine, but just for himself.

On the other hand, it was very annoying that it was
so easy for him to push her buttons and leave her
gasping for breath on the floor.

"Okay, well, you should know I'm anti-fur," she
said finally, her hands clenched into little fists as she
paced back and forth. "So, naked in sable or fully
clothed in sable—I'm against it."

He turned back from his camera bag, where he was
stowing equipment. "Got it. No fur. But you know,
Mabel, you could try faux sable. It would look great
with your hair."

"It would?"

He glanced up. "Absolutely."

Naked in faux sable. She melted. She had this vision of herself in nothing but a soft, fuzzy coat, spread out on the floor, while Trace—

Yikes! Get a grip! It was just a job for him, nothing more. She already knew about his vow not to get involved with people he worked with, but apparently this incessant teasing didn't count. Flirting like crazy must be okay as long as you both knew it wasn't going anywhere. Which was nice for him, but awful for her, since she had never learned to flirt properly.

She paced in the other direction, her hands fisted on her hips, watching him pack away film canisters and lenses, fold away his tripod. "So, Trace?"

"Yeah?"

Why did you want a shot of me like that? Instead, she asked, "Did you get what you needed for the 'before' pictures?"

"We'll have to see what they turn out like, but, yeah, I think so. The black-and-white shots against the wall should work fine. The rest of it was just for fun." He shrugged, and a hint of a smile played around his lips. "What can I say? I have a hard time looking at wonderful stuff through the lens and not shooting it. I mean, it may not work for this, but you can't turn down opportunity when it knocks on your lens cap."

"Oh, I see." Wonderful stuff through the lens? That would be *her?* Mabel wondered if her head was swelling. "Uh, Trace?"

He sat back on the floor, giving her his full regard. "Yes, Mabel?"

"Well, I wanted to know..."

He waited. After a long moment, during which Mabel chewed on her thumbnail and mentally tussled with how to complete that thought, Trace finally asked, "Mabel? What is it you're trying to ask?"

I'd like to ask you to please stop looking at me with those bedroom eyes because it makes me unable to form a coherent thought.

Now where had *that* come from?

"Mabel?" he prompted. "Question?"

Seized by an inspiration, she rushed out with, "I wanted to see what your opinion was, of what to do next. I know you don't want to plan the whole thing out in detail or anything, but what about just one step?"

At last he turned that impossible gaze away, this time rummaging in the pockets of his leather jacket for film. "I think it's pretty cut-and-dried. No planning required. But I suppose that's up to you."

"Up to me? Really?" So far, that wasn't working. She still had no idea where to begin. "Are you sure you don't want to toss out an idea or two? After all, you're the expert. Not because of the camera, I mean, but because you're, well, you're just the sort of man any *Real Men* reader would love to attract."

This time, there was more than a touch of dry humor in his tone. "Oh, yeah?"

"Sure. Gorgeous, worldly, self-assured, talented…" Mabel stopped herself before she drooled all over him. *Stupid, stupid,* she told herself. Maybe "ho-hum" women spilled their guts, but "hot" women were supposed to keep their mouths shut. And if that wasn't on the list of tips, it should have been.

"I'm all that, huh? Maybe I should hire you to do PR for me."

"Yeah, right." She managed a scratchy laugh, and

then purposefully switched herself into a more busi-
nesslike mode. "Trace, I really would like to sit down
and make some kind of blueprint. The two of us."
He opened his mouth to respond, but she headed him
off at the pass. "Okay, wait. Not a big scheme or a
master plan, nothing to squelch anyone's sparks, but
just a start."

"I guess it won't hurt us to know what's next," he
allowed. Dropping into her rocking chair, he tugged
the folder across the coffee table toward him, then
leaned over to consider the top page. "So, we have
to go with these, huh?"

Blocking the animal-print thong from her mind,
Mabel bent in a little nearer to look over his shoulder,
but she wasn't reading the list. Instead, she was trac-
ing the strong angle of his shoulder, the long, hard
sinews in his arm....

Trace looked up suddenly. "Do you have a pair of
scissors?"

"Scissors? What do you want to cut?" She
clutched at the straight, light brown hair that brushed
her shoulders. "Is that on the list— 'Chop off your
mane, Jane'?"

"Your hair's safe," he assured her. "Jane gets
'Make love on a train.' Tip #39. The mane goes with
Elaine. It's #16—'Put streaks in your mane, Elaine.'
So no chopping. What about the scissors?"

Mabel retreated to fetch them, still in the dark.
When she handed them over, Trace immediately set
about slicing the list into thin strips.

"What are you doing? That's my only copy," she
protested, trying to catch the paper slips as they fell
to the floor, already thinking about where she'd left
the tape.

"That's better," he muttered, tugging bits of paper away from her and starting to shuffle them into jumbled piles. "See? If you put the red hair together with the dramatic makeup, the tight dress, and the stiletto heels, it starts to make sense."

"It does?"

"Yeah. To me." He took a hard look at the thin sliver of paper in his hand. "Whereas the leather thing—"

"What leather thing?" she demanded.

"Tip #33." He pitched that slip onto one of his stacks. "'Wrap yourself in leather, Heather.' It's right here. Anyway, that goes better with the miniskirt, the B-52 hair and the sixties eyeliner."

Mabel sat down on the couch, not even bothering to try to understand what he was doing. She felt as if she were being assaulted on a whole bunch of levels, all at once. First, he teased her and caught her off-balance man-to-woman. And then he started playing with paper and scissors and made a mess in her apartment!

Desire, disorder... The things she was most uncomfortable with. What next?

"Think of it this way," he said patiently. "Like a series of smaller makeovers instead of one huge one. You can do these for a Biker Chick look." He tapped the stack with Heather's leather on top, his gaze drifting carelessly over Mabel, brushing her face, her lips, lingering on her legs. "Ever have a hankering to strap yourself onto a Harley, Mabel?"

She closed her eyes. "Not in this lifetime."

He went on, in that same soft, maddening, smug tone. "I think you'd love it."

"Picking bugs out of my hair and gravel out of my teeth? I don't think so."

"Okay," he allowed. "If you're not in the Biker Chick mood, you can go for the Starlet thing, with the hennaed hair and the skimpy dress, like you're on your way to a casting couch. That's this pile."

Strapped onto a Harley, casting couch... She couldn't listen to any more of this.

Mabel dropped back into the sofa, her head against the arm, exactly the position she'd had before he got here and confused things. "I still don't get how this helps us organize my story," she complained. "So what if we've now got a Biker Chick and a Starlet on a couch? How do we start?"

"Oh, this has nothing to do with starting. It's just for fun."

"I hate fun," she reflected.

"Mabel, Mabel, Mabel." He tossed the rest of the folder over onto her lap. "Okay, I'll help you out. You want a first step? Couldn't be easier. First, we take you to one of the salons on the other list, the one with 'recommended merchants,' or whatever Sophia called it. Find one you like. They put goop on your face, they cut and color your hair, they polish your nails, yadda, yadda, yadda."

A bona fide next step! Mabel latched on to that. Except... "Going to a spa isn't one of the tips. A regular 'ho-hum' person who wanted to follow the fifty ways wouldn't be able to just throw herself on the mercy of Elizabeth Arden."

"Too bad. If we take you there, we can kill a bunch of these helpful hints with one stone. So we're doing it." He lifted his shoulders in a careless shrug. "I'll take the pictures of you with mud on your face and some lady buffing your nails, and you write the first entry in your Makeover Diary, all about how much fun it was.''

This was actually doable. And it wasn't even gross. Mabel sat up and started to make notes on her clean legal pad. "Okay, so first, you took Plain Jane 'before' pictures.'' She wrote that down and then made a big, black check next to it. "Second, salon.'' She gazed at him expectantly. "And then?''

"After the salon? Well, we'll have to go shopping.'' Under his breath, he added, "Torture for me, heaven for you. Every girlfriend I ever had told me that when the going gets tough, the tough go shopping.''

"I hate shopping.''

Trace lifted a dark brow. "You hate fun *and* you hate shopping? Somebody needs to rock your world, honey.''

And you're just the guy to do it. She shook her head to clear away thoughts like that one. "You said it yourself,'' she maintained. "Shopping is torture. For me, too.''

"You can put that into your story.'' His tone was light, but definitely mocking. "All about how you had the incredible burden of walking into Chicago's finest boutiques and department stores with an expense account. Poor you.''

"You don't know what it's like,'' she returned, shaking her head. "I went into one of those fancy stores once. Something Italian. Fredo, Frodo? I don't know. The clerks were following me around, all grumpy, like they wanted to make sure I wouldn't breathe on anything.''

"Prada. This time I guarantee you'll get great service." His mouth curved into a lopsided smile. "This time you'll be with me."

And saleswomen would be eating out of his hand....

Although she didn't really want to give in, Mabel realized this shopping thing had to be done. Besides, she was tougher than some silly salesclerk in a boutique. Raising her chin, she asked, "So what are we going to buy?"

"It makes sense to me to start from the bottom up," he offered.

"B-bottom up, like shoes? Or tattoos?" she asked, not sure she wanted to hear the answer.

"Bottom, as in what goes under your clothes." He nabbed a piece of paper so far unassigned to any pile and waved it at her. "As in, 'Buy lingerie, Kay.'"

Oh, no. Mabel swallowed around a dry throat. Was that the one with the dreaded animal-print thong?

"I'm not ready for that yet. Not, uh, underwear," she said quickly. She couldn't manage the word *lingerie* in front of him, let alone *thong*. "I think I'd rather look at dresses first. I mean, that makes sense, because how can you know what should go under it until you have it? The dress, I mean. Straps, strapless, short, long, can you wear black under it? You have to have the dress first because otherwise you might totally screw up the, uh, foundation."

"You'd know more about that than I would," he said with a sardonic edge.

Somehow she doubted it. But at least he was derailed from the lingerie track. For the time being. That look in his eyes was very suspicious.

Mabel went back to her pad. "Okay, so I have, number one, 'Before' Pictures, and I've marked it done. Number two, Spa or Salon for Hair and Makeup and Whatever Else They Do There.'' She glanced up. ''Number three, Clothes. I guess I'll need more than one dress, huh? I mean, what with leather and black lace and...'' Trailing off, she blew out a deep breath. ''And whatever else is on that horrifying list of tips.''

She told herself the pictures of her in totally unsuitable garments would at least be humorous.

''Don't forget to write down number four, Racy Underwear,'' Trace said with a great deal of innocence that she had a hard time believing.

She hated this. She really hated this. But she wrote ''lingerie'' next to the number four, even if it did come out a little wobbly.

''All right, then,'' he said, rising from the rocker, leaving his little piles of paper slips littered on her coffee table. He grabbed his leather jacket up off the floor, and headed to where he'd dropped his camera bag. ''I'll pick you up first thing in the morning and we'll be off to whatever salon you choose.''

Mabel jumped to her feet. ''Wait! You can't just leave like this.''

His gaze flickered over the room. ''Aren't we done?''

''There are only four things on my list!'' She tried frantically to think of some good reason to keep him, afraid to be left alone with her panic. ''And you made a mess by dicing up all fifty 'Ways to Lure Your Lover' and dumping them there.''

His beautiful blue eyes, so lushly framed by those deep black lashes, held her, steady and unmoved. ''You and I both know you'll have it all taped back together before I make it to my car.''

''Well, no, actually, I thought I might rewrite the

original list, and then type up a new one, or, that is, a new set of lists, with the tips divided into sections corresponding to the piles you made,'' she said awkwardly. ''Kind of cross-reference it.''

He opened the door to let himself out, turning back to send her a wry smile. ''Why am I not surprised?''

''Do we need a reservation?'' she called after him. ''Tomorrow, for the salon?''

''Naw. Remember, you'll be with me.''

And then he and his damn blue eyes were gone, leaving Mabel alone with her Benedict Arnold of a cat and a heap of shredded paper.

She might as well get to work. The disarray on her coffee table was making her itchy, plus she had a big day ahead of her. After all, getting made over into a vixen was tough work.

''But somebody has to do it,'' she said out loud.

MABEL BEGAN HER MORNING by perusing the list of salons on Sophia Weston's list over an untouched bowl of Grape Nuts.

Oddly enough, after a little research, she was starting to get excited by this spa idea. A little guilty, but excited. After going back and forth, she finally chose the Coquille Day Spa on ultrachic Oak Street, just off Chicago's Magnificent Mile. And then she sat back and imagined herself emerging from her salon experience as a whole new woman.

She smiled. Except then she happened to glance at the clock and almost fainted from the rush of adrenaline. Trace would be here any minute to pick her up! In a rush, she stumbled to get dressed. What did you wear on an ''undercover odyssey,'' anyway? Mabel settled on a plain white shirt and tan pants. Very "makeover-able."

The doorbell rang just as she fluffed her hair and wondered whether it was impolite to wear no makeup to a makeover.

"Hi," she said brightly, wrenching open the door and practically rolling over Trace in her eagerness to get going.

He eyed her strangely as they took the stairs. "What's up with all the enthusiasm?"

"I'm starting to get psyched." She beamed at him. "I've never really had the chance to experience life as, I don't know, a suburban society girl, popping up to Oak Street for a facial and a manicure. I think I might like it."

Trace didn't say anything, just steered her toward his rented BMW. Mabel wasn't sure what to make of his silence, but she was too caught up in the Cinderella fantasy to mind much.

Before she knew it, he'd deposited her at the spa— a posh, intimate place, decorated mostly in white, with a few peachy swirls on the wall in the vague shape of seashells. Thick towels, hushed tones, the smell of sea spray, and the sound of waves crashing on some unseen shore set the mood.

Mabel figured this was supposed to be soothing, but Trace must have told the Coquille staff that they were on a timetable. She was whipped from one chair to the next, from manicure to pedicure to seaweed wrap, with no chance whatsoever to ask Trace what he thought of her smoky eye makeup or her new, witchy fingernails. He was there in the background, snapping away, but he seemed a lot more distant than he had last night.

Still, she found herself grinning like a fool throughout the whole thing. Why, it was fun to be fussed over! Of course, she kept having to stop them, to write down the details, but they didn't seem to mind.

Jean-Paul, the salon's top stylist, and Jean-Claude, the makeup expert, were happy as clams to be doing a makeover for *Real Men,* and to have the famous Mr. Cameron recording their handiwork for posterity.

"Gorgeous! You are exquisite!" Jean-Claude kept telling her, with an accent that was so thick it had to be fake. She was guessing his real name was Clyde and he'd come straight from Hinckley-Big Rock High School or someplace like it; but, hey, who was she to complain about pretending to be something you weren't?

For today, Jean-Paul had lightened her hair a little and cut it into more of a shag and less of a bob, while Jean-Claude had gone with sexy city-girl makeup. Or at least that was what they told her, as Mabel took copious notes. She also had instructions on how to accomplish various other items on the list, and she furiously scribbled information into her notebook.

After much giggling and laughing, Jean-Paul blew her hair and its new streaky gold highlights into carefree wisps, and voilà! pronounced her finished.

"Hmm…" She squinted at herself in the mirror. "Who the heck are *you?*"

Raspberry sea-salt facial, rosemary shampoo, violet clarifying lotion, persimmon exfoliator, cucumber eye revitalizer… Feeling a bit like she ought to be an entrée on the lunch menu, Mabel emerged about two hours after she'd arrived, with a new hairdo and makeup, but back in her tan pants and white shirt. She was toting three big bags of beauty products she was supposed to be able to create marvelous effects with at home. She was under no illusions that they would work, but at least it might be fun trying.

As she pushed through the doors, she gave Trace a big smile and a little twirl. "So?"

"So we have to get moving," he said impatiently, hauling her bags along with his camera equipment and rushing her out the door. "I thought we'd never get out of there."

He was awfully grumpy. And hadn't made even one comment about her finished appearance.

She allowed herself a moment to feel cheated. It wasn't every day a girl got a whole new look. Someone ought to notice! But Trace strode ahead of her, other men streamed by on all sides, and no one batted an eye.

So far, she concluded, she must be stuck back at "sedate," with "seductive" nowhere to be found. In mid-step, she pulled out her omnipresent notebook and scrawled in it.

New hair and makeup. No apparent change in relative hotness. No men noticing.

Trace stopped on a dime. "What are you writing now?"

"Oh, you know. Observations," she said vaguely. Just then, her stomach growled loudly, reminding her that she'd forgotten to eat her breakfast in her excitement to begin this project. She ventured, "Can we stop somewhere for lunch now? I'm starved."

"You want to eat before you try on tiny dresses?" He frowned. "Mabel, what sense does that make?"

Since they were right next to three or four chichi

clothing boutiques, she supposed it didn't make sense to go somewhere else to find food and then come right back. Still, her stomach was rumbling.

"Being streaked and exfoliated is hard work," she muttered. "And I don't see what you're so cranky about, anyway."

"You can have a snack as soon as we get your clothes. Come on. I just want to get this over with."

"I'm sorry my company is such a burden," she said stiffly. What was wrong with him? He'd been so charming and fun before, even if he was a little too sexy for anyone's good. But from the first moment he'd seen her this morning, he'd acted like he had a thorn in his paw.

"Sorry," he said darkly. "It's not your company. It's just…"

"What?"

"Nothing." He picked up his pace, but Mabel pulled him back.

"Tell me. There's obviously something wrong."

He waited for a long moment, still moody. Finally, he muttered, "I thought you were different. All of a sudden, you're acting like all the other beauty-obsessed women I've known. If you're wise, you won't turn into one of them. Trust me."

Mabel rolled her eyes. "Please. You just liked me when I was acting scared and nerdy, so you could tease me and drive me nuts. Not to mention you could push me around."

His smile was slow. "Well, yeah."

"Well, too bad. You're the one who told me to lighten up and have fun." She lifted her shoulders. "So I am."

His eyes narrowed. He didn't say anything, but she saw the challenge there. *Let's see how long this lasts.*

"Okay, so how about this one?" She gestured to the door of the Sonia Rykiel shop, where she could see some very smart knit dresses.

"Much too dignified. I read the list, remember?" Trace grabbed Mabel's hand and pulled her along to something called Jane Kuku, where the window was full of loud prints, spandex, and even a few feathers.

"Eeeeuw."

"Jane Kuku is fun and fresh, and all of her designs are very body-conscious, which is exactly what you need." Trace pushed open the door, just as if he were laying down a dare. "Come on in, Mabel."

She lagged behind him, not at all ready for this. Makeup was one thing, but this was The Big Step: baring her bod. She knew very well what she looked like in normal pants and tops, in suits and loose dresses. But the stuff the magazine had in mind... Was she really brave enough?

If Trace liked her better shaking in her boots, he might just be getting his wish.

"Are you sure we can't eat lunch first? What's the rush? Do you have to be somewhere or something? And what does 'body-conscious' mean, anyway?"

"It means 'tight.' Mabel, stop stalling. It won't be that bad."

"I'm not stalling," she said indignantly.

He just grinned at her. Yep, she could tell he was starting to like her better already, now that she was nervous. She wasn't in this to please him. In fact, *not* pleasing him sounded pretty good just now.

Confidence, Mabel, she told herself. *You can do this.*

"Okay, so what do we need?" Trace fished a crumpled piece of paper out of his pocket. She recognized it as his copy of her newly typed list. He'd only had it for an hour or so, and already it was crumpled. *Really.*

"'Something clingy, something red, something with a low neckline, something short, something in see-through black lace, something in leather...'" He glanced up at Mabel with a twinkle in his eye. "This is like a scavenger hunt."

"Yeah, the call girl's scavenger hunt. What a concept."

Trace gave her another one of his long, intense stares. "Mabel, you couldn't look like a call girl if we stuck you nude on the Kennedy Expressway at rush hour."

"I could if I wanted to," she retorted. "I just wouldn't want to. Not nude, on the Kennedy." She considered. "Maybe the Eisenhower."

His tone was mocking. "Uh-huh."

"So, do you guys need help or something?" interrupted a salesgirl whose outfit seemed to match most of the categories they were looking for. The girl had a pout and a bad attitude, until she saw Trace lift his camera with its long lens and point it her way. Then she straightened, pushed out her chest, tossed her hair and smiled big. "Wow, so what is this for? I'm Gigi, by the way, and you know, anything you need, it's like, *yours.*"

Trace explained their *Real Men* mission, and then gave Gigi a hefty tip to lock the front door so they could have the store to themselves for a little while. As she scurried to comply, he steered Mabel toward a wallful of what looked like Halloween costumes.

"Okay, let me see," the clerk said helpfully, pawing through the racks. "Hmm... Okay, well, this blouse might be good. It's black lace, lots of cleavage, and goes with this leather miniskirt." She held up two hangers to form an outfit that didn't have enough fabric for a normal bathing suit.

"I would rather see something a little different," Mabel began, putting up her hands to ward the thing off.

"I like it." Trace held it up in front of Mabel, calling her bluff, fitting it to the front of her, and she had no choice but to take it. "Is there a leather jacket, too? Preferably one with lots of zippers? You don't sell thigh-high boots, do you?"

"You've got to be kidding!" Mabel protested, but he tilted down very close to her ear and murmured, "Wild, Mabel. Think wild."

"I'm trying," she managed. "Do they have anything with more fabric?"

But Trace handed her another tiny piece of cloth, this one a stretchy skirt littered with red and black flowers, along with a couple of other things she couldn't even identify.

"Oooh," the girl said. "That shiny silver one, the Lycra minidress, is going to look so hot on you."

"Thank you. I think."

"He's really good at this stuff," the salesgirl confided to Mabel. "Most guys are like a pain in the butt, but he knows just what to pick out."

Mabel's head began to swim as she took in her armload of skimpy clothes. She could have handled "low-cut," a brief hemline, even "clingy"—one at a time. But all at once? It made her see stars. "I guess he's got a good eye," she muttered grimly.

"He's got a good everything," the salesclerk returned with a giggle.

There was that. Mabel had been trying not to think about it. But the man was so damn good-looking. Today he had on khakis with a black knit shirt, and that same worn leather jacket with film canisters and lens caps falling out of the pockets. Nice. Not fancy, just *right*, the way the pants clung to his hips and flowed over his...

He turned then, and caught her looking.

He didn't say a word, just raised a dark eyebrow, as if he knew exactly what she was thinking. And he gave her a devilish smile.

A very naughty thought popped into her head before she had a chance to stop it. What would he do if she cast away her load of fashion nightmares, grabbed him, and rolled him under the racks for a couple of hours?

Totally inappropriate. Totally stupid. But her mouth went dry just the same. *What would he do?*

"What are you waiting for?" he asked.

"'Waiting'? 'For'?" She froze. Was he reading her mind again? Did he *want* her to toss away the clothes and grab him?

He nodded at the garments in her arms. "Are you going to try those on, Mabel?" he asked, his eyes alive with mischief. "Or do you want me to find a few more?"

"No!" She gazed down at her collection of slinky dresses and scandalous separates. If she was already melting when all he did was look at her, fully clothed, what the heck would she do when she had to prance around in these wicked things? This was torture.

Breathless, she mumbled, "I guess I have to try them on."

"Gigi," he said, abruptly switching focus, "how would you feel about going out for a little while, long enough for us to shoot some pictures here in the store?"

"I don't think I can—"

But Trace reached for his wallet, and that took care of the salesclerk's objections. He turned back to Mabel with a dark smile. "Total privacy and a storeful of clothes. Looks like you're up."

Oh, he was enjoying this, wasn't he? "Hey, I just had a better idea. I could buy them and take them home," she said in a rush, "and, you know, put them on there, in front of my very own mirror, and whatever didn't work, I could bring back—"

"We need to shoot this, here, for the article. A fashion parade is probably the most important thing, don't you think?" he asked sweetly, steering her inexorably toward a try-on room.

She couldn't think of a single rebuttal. It appeared there was no way to get out of this with her pride intact.

Trace leaned in and lowered his voice. "Mabel, time to put up or shut up."

"Okay, okay." She took a step forward, faltered, stopped, and started to retreat—

But Trace was right behind her.

No turning back now. Wondering how in the heck she'd gotten herself into this mess, Mabel murmured, "Damn the hot pants, full speed ahead.

4

Tip #44: Make the boy wait, Kate.

Anticipation. Heightened awareness. That's
what it's all about. Whether it's your entrance
for a date or the first time you make love, you'll
be surprised how much power there is in pro-
longing the suspense.

"MABEL, WHAT'S TAKING so long?" Trace paced
back and forth outside the dressing room, jiggling his
camera in one hand. "You must have something on
by now."

"Uh, no. Not yet."

Her voice was low and barely audible, and he felt
like storming right into her little room and seeing
what exactly she was hiding. She'd had plenty of time
to try on every single one of those "body-conscious"
outfits, and they both knew it. He never should have
let her go in there by herself, after it was clear she
was dragging her feet. He should have known she'd
stage some kind of sit-down strike.

Meanwhile, he cooled his heels and fumed. If it
were any other woman, any normal model, he would
have been phoning *Real Men* for a replacement, giv-

ing Sophia Weston a piece of his mind about wasting his time.

But for Mabel...he'd wait.

"Chump," he muttered, shaking his head at his own folly.

What was it about Mabel, anyway? She amused him, he knew that. He liked the fact that she was feisty and funny and different from anyone he knew. Smart, definitely. A little naive. But always surprising.

Something about her pushed him to annoy and pester and get a rise out of her, as if she spoke directly to the seven-year-old hiding inside him, the one who couldn't resist chasing little girls with worms.

And then sometimes she just plain drove him up a wall.

"Mabel," he tried again, "I'm not the most patient guy in the world. Put something on and get out here, or I'm coming in there."

"No!" she cried immediately.

He stepped closer, purposely making his footfalls loud enough to rattle her door.

"You can't come in." She opened up a sliver, poking out her tousled head. He could see the panic in her wide, hazel eyes, and he softened. She really was cute when she was in a tizzy. "You can't... I mean, I still haven't managed to..."

And then she swore and slammed the door shut.

"Mabel," he said sternly, smacking his palm flat against the wooden barrier. "Out. Now."

"No."

He tried the knob, but she was clearly leaning against it, blocking the way. Okay, so maybe he should try a different tack.

In a soft, sweet, soothing tone, he murmured, "It can't be that bad. Come on, you can show me."

"I don't have anything to show you," she retorted. "These stupid fingernails have made everything impossible. I could hardly get my own clothes off, and then all these goofy fabrics, with flimsy lace and spandex and I-don't-know-what... I keep getting my nails caught on everything, and I can't even do a zipper. As if it weren't bad enough to have to model these dippy clothes, now I can't even dress myself!"

Trace tried very hard not to laugh.

"I'm stuck!" she continued in the same furious tone. "Halfway in and halfway out! And don't tell me to take the idiotic nails off because I tried that and I almost ripped my whole thumb off instead."

"Sorry about the thumb." He wiggled the doorknob one more time. "But I can help, Mabel. I can fasten you up."

There was a pause. "How?" she asked finally. "You are not coming in here with me!"

An old trick came easily to his lips. "Open the door a couple of inches and I'll reach in. I won't look. Promise."

Silence hung there for several seconds.

"Mabel," he reminded her, "you have to come out sometime. I suppose I could pass you food and water for a couple of hours, but the management is probably going to draw the line after that."

"Okay," she said with what was either a growl or a groan. "I suppose I don't have any choice."

The door squeaked open about three inches.

"But you'd better not look or I swear I'll kill you."

He slipped his left hand in around the crack, reaching for anything that felt like Mabel. All he got was air. "Where are you?"

"I have to..." There was a rustling, scrunching noise. "I got it twisted. I'm going to have to wrestle— Oops."

Wrestle? He had a sudden, crystal-clear mental image of that process, and his palms began to sweat.

But then he heard a clunk and Mabel fell against his hand briefly, before she righted herself. "Sorry. I kind of lost my balance," she said quickly. "Try again."

More rustling and scrunching and muttered oaths. Those sounds were very intriguing. Very. Trace clenched his jaw. Was she doing this on purpose? It was like a striptease, only upside-down and backward. And he was dying out here.

"Okay," she told him finally. "I'm ready for your part."

Smooth, warm, very bare skin brushed his outstretched hand. Her shoulder? Maybe the slope of her neck. God, he wanted to look. Gently, he skimmed his fingers an inch or two along her skin, feeling the need to identify where he was. But she squealed and grabbed his hand the second it moved.

"Hey, no groping!"

"I'm not groping," he said curtly. "This isn't exactly easy, you know. You try playing blind man's bluff around a door."

"You try doing fasteners with three-inch claws," she returned. "Okay, are you ready? I put on the black one, the two-piece, with the— Oh, never mind. I got the skirt mostly on, except for the zipper. And I have the top on, but it's open all the way down the back. It buttons. Can you do that?"

Open down the back. "I, uh—" Open all the way down the back? What in the hell was she trying to do to him?

"Here," she said, guiding his hand down to her waist. "Just zip this up first."

He slid his hand around her hip, deciphering the terrain.

"Trace," she warned. "If you're trying to be funny…"

"I'm not," he protested. Gingerly, trying to ignore the layer of perspiration breaking out on his brow, he edged his fingers along until they grazed the teeth of the zipper. He felt thin, raw silk, stretching against Mabel's curves, and he knew that lower down, that round mound would fit his hand like nobody's business.

His hand was going to start shaking if this kept up. *Concentrate,* he told himself. *This is Mabel. Goofy, klutzy Mabel. She's no siren.*

So why were so many alarms going off in his brain?

"Hold down on your bottom, I mean, *the* bottom— the bottom of the skirt," he said gruffly. "I'll pull up the zipper."

It was tight, but he gritted his teeth and tugged. Zipped in. *Thank God.*

As if it had a mind of its own, his hand patted her derriere, ever so lightly.

"Trace!"

"Sorry. Just celebrating being halfway there."

"Okay." But her voice didn't sound okay. She sounded breathless, trembling… Turned-on.

This wasn't good. Another minute of this touchy-feely game, and he'd be kicking in the door, wrapping

Mabel in his arms, ripping off whatever it was he'd just zipped her into, and making love to her hard and fast against the wall of the dressing room.

Yeah, that was classy. Especially when he knew very well he had no business fooling around with Mabel, of all people. He'd already said he wouldn't, couldn't, get involved with someone he worked with.

And this was *Mabel* he was talking about. She projected innocence and inexperience. She was not the kind of woman with whom you shared hot, meaningless sex in a public place and then walked away. She'd be wounded. She'd misunderstand. Hell, she'd probably sue.

He pulled his hand back.

"Here's the, uh, top," she whispered, cozying up closer to the door. Through the crack, he could see inches of her creamy, pale skin, the gaping edges of the black lace crop top, a few tendrils of golden brown hair tickling the nape of her neck....

"There's no way I can button with one hand," he said more sharply than he'd intended. "Besides, you're mostly covered. You can come out."

Mabel wrenched open the door with a swoosh, holding the blouse to her front with both hands. Her cheeks were flushed, and her breath was a little ragged, as her eyes searched his. What was she looking for?

Trace held himself very still, doing his best to appear unaffected.

She whispered, "Don't laugh, okay?"

"Laugh?" What, was she nuts? "I'm not laughing."

"All right." She spun around. "So button already."

The lace top was stretchy and difficult to maneuver, and he had to pull hard to wrap the loops around the buttons. He could only imagine what he was tugging against on the front of her to mold the shirt to her body. Imagining... This was almost worse than when they'd had the door between them. He closed his eyes and buttoned her up so fast it was a blur.

"Done," he said bleakly.

"All right." Mabel scooted away from him, standing awkwardly in the revealing outfit, hugging one arm across her chest and tugging at her hemline with her other hand. "So where do you want me?"

Anywhere I can take you. "To shoot, you mean?"

She nodded.

"I, uh..." He hadn't remembered to think about it. This was bizarre. No matter what, everybody knew Trace Cameron delivered the pictures. Yet here he was, getting sidetracked by a dizzy, sassy neat-freak with a list fixation. Not exactly his type. He improvised with, "Why don't you pose on that platform up in front, the one with the mannequins?"

After inching around him, Mabel sped down the main aisle ahead of him, almost dancing with nerves and unease. His eyes followed, glued to her anatomy whether he liked it or not.

Mabel was small and slim, but she'd been hidden under baggy clothes every time he'd seen her. He'd never have guessed how amazing she'd look in these hot little clothes. Cut down to there in the front and up to...*there* at the hem, the outfit should have been illegal.

As she hoisted herself up onto the blocks next to a couple of scantily clad mannequins, the shiny black skirt bound her like shrink-wrap, and when she bent one way or angled the other, her bottom looked firm and round and delicious. Incorrigible, he closed in on it with his zoom lens.

"I should've let you stay in there," he murmured under his breath. "'Sight unseen.'"

"What did you say?"

Automatically, he came up with a cover. "I said, duck under the mannequin. The one in the red jacket. Like she has her arm around you. Good. Turn around so you're facing me straight on." *And I don't have to look at your adorable backside in that damn skirt.*

But now he had the front view, which was almost as bad. Her small, perfect breasts filled out the confining, low-cut neckline, and her legs looked slender and long under the brief skirt.

He knew he was hiding behind the camera, but he did it anyway, snapping picture after picture, accelerating to a frantic rhythm.

"Turn, spin, breathe," he commanded, moving her around the store, putting her through her paces, never once touching her. "Over this way more. Tip your chin up. Look into the mirror. Your hand on your hip. Good. Great. One more. Lean toward me. Chin up." He had a full, unobstructed view of her breasts. God, it was good.

He felt his face flaming with heat, and he saw her lips part as she gasped for breath. He was making love to her with the camera, and they both knew it.

"Okay," he said finally, drawing back. As Mabel stood there, a little wobbly but unscathed, Trace ran a shaky hand through his hair. What the hell had he done?

In his career, he'd taken photos of supermodels topless in the sand and movie stars wearing nothing but dabs of paint, but it was funny little Mabel in a tight dress who had him on his knees. Go figure.

"Hey, are you guys done?" It was Gigi, back from her break, just in the nick of time to save his soul.

"Not quite. But that's okay. You can stay." He needed a chaperon. Big time. "Gigi, why don't you go back to the dressing room with Mabel? She's having some trouble with her fingernails. Do you mind helping her change?"

"Hey, no problem."

With Gigi's help, Mabel was able to get in and out of her clothes in a jiffy. She waltzed back and forth in leather and Lycra, in purple plastic pants and a backless dress that revealed more than it covered, putting on the fashion show they needed for the pages of *Real Men.*

Trace had to practically recite the Gettysburg Address to keep himself cool, collected, uninvolved. But he could see Mabel gaining confidence with each outfit, vamping just a little more, slyly gauging the impact she was making. Now she was so happy she was humming something. What was it? "Girls Just Want to Have Fun"?

He'd created a monster.

Mabel was going to eat him alive, like Godzilla chomping his way through the Metropolitan Life Building. Unless he was very, very careful.

"I think we have plenty on film," he said, concentrating on unscrewing his lens, not looking at her. "If you want to put your own clothes back on, we can get on to the next stop."

"Sounds good." She wafted past him, leaning in closer. "You do remember what's next, don't you?"

He didn't take the bait. "You were pretty anxious for lunch, as I recall."

"Undies," she breathed. "I can't wait."

Trace held himself firmly in check. He felt like spanking her, but considering the fact that she was wearing spandex hot pants, he didn't trust himself to turn her over his knee.

Still, as she changed into her street clothes, he knew he was going to have to do something. And then he knew what. Okay, so it was low. He was desperate to defuse Mabel.

So when she came back, demure in her chinos and white button-down shirt, he was all smiles.

She narrowed her eyes, clearly suspicious of his change in mood. Well, that was the idea. Keep her off-balance. Annoy the heck out of her. Put the ball back in *his* court.

"Gigi, can you ring these up?" Mabel asked, lumping a few outfits into the salesgirl's arms, but keeping her gaze on Trace.

"So which ones did you decide to take?"

"A little of this, a little of that," she said absently. "Nothing I'd ever wear normally, of course, but I have to have something to test. You know, when I 'walk on the wild side,' as Sophia would put it."

"Oh, yeah. Speaking of Sophia, I have a new tip for you, Mabel." He gave her a purposely naughty smile. "Remember 'Get naked in sable, Mabel'?"

She groaned, and he saw the old Mabel return in that blink of an eye. "Sable," she snapped, her shoulders squaring, color rising on her cheeks. "Yuck. How could I forget?"

"Well, I've got another one for you."

Mabel started to walk away to pick up her packages.

"'Watch porn on cable, Mabel.' How do you like it?"

She spun around, her eyes wide. "'Watch porn on cable'? Eeeuw! That is so gross. Why in the world would you say that?"

He shrugged. To annoy her, obviously.

Mabel shook her head, setting her lips in a firm, disgusted line. "Porn on cable," she said again. "I don't think so!"

Trace smiled to himself as he stowed his equipment. He had her number. She might get a kick out of feeling frisky for a minute or two, but give her a chance to act high-minded and stuffy, and she'd grab it every time.

But he wasn't out of the woods yet. Next stop, the WispyWear Boutique. Could Mabel take the heat? Could he?

Thinking ahead to stage two of their shopping and shooting expedition, to this newer, bolder Mabel getting ahold of camisoles and corsets, Trace realized there was one thing he desperately needed.

Ice cubes.

IT ONLY TOOK ONE LOOK in the window of the lingerie store to change her mind.

"Okay, so I do want lunch first," Mabel announced. *Good heavens.* The stuff was really seedy. Even for the process of experimentation, even after the heady success at the Kuku boutique, she wasn't ready for *that.*

"Fine with me." He agreed so quickly it confused her, but she let him nudge her around the corner onto

Michigan Avenue. "There's a deli I like a few blocks down, on Chestnut. That okay?"

She'd never heard of Chestnut Street. When had he suddenly turned into Mr. Map? "How do you know about delis on Chestnut Street? I thought you just flew in from New York for this shoot." She suddenly had this mental image of him as a wee tot, being rolled down the Magnificent Mile in his gold-plated pram. "Don't tell me, you were born and raised at Lake Point Tower, and you know the posh parts of the city like the back of your hand."

"No. I've never been here before. Born and raised in New Jersey."

"New Jersey?" How odd. She hated it when he blew her stereotypes. "So?" she prodded. "When did you learn street names and restaurants? Shooting Cindy Crawford at Michael Jordan's restaurant?"

"I said I'd never been here before." He glanced a block ahead. "*Real Men* put me up at the Ritz, right over there. If I'm in a strange city, I like to know the lay of the land. Or at least the lay of a few blocks and a good deli."

"The Ritz?" she echoed wistfully, thinking of her own meager apartment in its dicey neighborhood. So they were equal partners in this deal, huh? It appeared some people's expense accounts went a lot deeper than others'.

"Maybe I'm worth it," he said with a smoky glance.

No comment. She followed along as he led her to a small deli with dark tables and wonderful odors. As soon as they walked in, her stomach rumbled like a lion at the zoo, reacting to the smell of pastrami and chopped liver.

Roar. There it was again, even louder.

He arched an eyebrow. "Do you always sound like that?"

"Only when I'm starving." After stuffing all her Kuku and Coquille parcels in and around an empty chair, she grabbed the menu and started to scan the columns. If she were honest, she'd admit she didn't care what she ate as long as it came quickly and gave her something to do besides stare at him and wonder what he'd really been thinking when she was trying on those clothes at Kuku.

She'd have been the first to admit it: She was a fish out of water in all these new places. When you grew up in central Illinois, in a town with a total population of 312—counting a few pigs and cows—you knew the big city was going to be scary. Sure, she'd been class valedictorian, editor of the school newspaper, and a fine second baseman on the softball team. But none of that had prepared her for college, let alone life as a single professional woman in Chicago.

From the beginning, Mabel had refused to be cowed. She had always forged right ahead, taking her new experiences where she found them.

Still, prancing around in skimpy, bizarre outfits in front of someone worldly-wise and sophisticated like Trace Cameron was undoubtedly the weirdest thing she'd ever done. She didn't know whether to be proud or embarrassed that she'd actually started to like it there at the end.

Over her menu, she said aloud, "Wonder whether the chicken salad is good," but she was thinking, *I know I saw a light in his eyes. I know he was attracted to me. How can that be? I'm the total Plain*

Jane package, after all. No way the likes of him goes for Plain Jane.

But I know what I saw.

Or did she?

She gave him a searching look over her menu, and got a similar one right back from him. Jeez Louise, he was hard to figure. She couldn't remember ever in her life wishing she were a mind reader, but today was the day.

Quickly, she dropped her gaze back to the columns of pickled herring and matzo balls.

If she brooded over this anymore, she was going to lose it completely. The waiter sidled up, and Mabel hastened to pick something from the menu. Then she dragged out her notebook, bent on recording her conflicted thoughts.

"What are you writing now?" he asked, with a hint of ill temper.

"I told you before, these are my observations." Chewing on her pen, she concentrated on the page.

Plain Jane—PJ—noted definite increase in seductiveness when wearing clothing listed in tips. Closest male seemed affected, although results inconclusive. Once PJ back in regular clothing, man in question—MIQ—reverted to previous aggravating behavior.

She frowned.

Also, MIQ is really driving PJ bananas, although PJ is unsure how that fits into any of this.

She went back and crossed that out, but it made her feel less frustrated to have written it down. Then

she jotted down a few other things she'd learned during her try-on phase. A sudden inspiration hit, and
she added a note.

PJ should not apply fingernails until *after* trying
on clothing.

"Thank goodness Gigi knew how to get those stupid things off," she muttered, examining her bare,
pink nails. "I would've been hobbled for life."

"Are you going to get them put back on?"

Once again, he had the funniest look in his eye,
and Mabel couldn't help remembering the tip about
"claws." *"One look at your untamed fingernails, and
he'll be unable to think of anything but the tracks
you'll leave on his back."*

Well, that couldn't be it. Not Trace. "Trace?"

"Yeah?" But he was still staring at her fingernails.

"Trace, did those long, red fingernails make you
think of anything in particular?" she inquired
thoughtfully.

He frowned. "That women are nuts to have them
if they can't even button themselves," he said
abruptly. He made a point of going back to his menu.

"Okay," she said with a shrug. Just as she'd
thought. The last thing on his mind was anyone
scratching his back. "That tip was bogus. I have to
write that down."

With that taken care of, she resurrected her To Do
list. There was still nothing after number four, Lingerie, but she had a clearer mental picture of the next
steps now that she'd seen the proposed clothing items.

"We're back on that, are we?" he inquired, putting

aside his menu and trying to read upside down from his side of the table. "Mabel's Master Makeover Plan."

She sat up straighter and gave him her cheeriest smile. "Yes, but now I know what I want to do after I dispose of the lingerie."

Trace suddenly grabbed his water glass and gulped down a big swallow. Then he began to crunch on an ice cube. Mabel eyed him curiously. What was that all about? Immediate onset of some incredible thirst?

He really did behave oddly sometimes.

Shaking her head, she ignored his awful munching sounds and went back to her pad. "To truly test that I've gone from 'ho-hum' to 'hot'…" She amended, "Not now, I mean, but after I put on the suggested outfits and makeup and shoes and all that. Anyway, to test this theory that the makeover will make men pant over me, I have to decide who it is I want to pant."

The chomping noise picked up in speed and volume.

Mabel narrowed her gaze. Was he trying to distract her? Or did he have some deep-seated need to gnaw on ice cubes like a bored teenager at the multiplex? She frowned. "I think," she decided, "that my target should be someone I already know."

"Like who?" he asked quickly.

Well, at least he was paying attention. "I'm getting to that. Like I said, to truly test this before-and-after thing, it has to be someone who has seen me *before*. Otherwise I won't be able to judge if *after* makes a difference."

She thought her reasoning was brilliant, but Trace didn't say a word. Tapping her pen against the paper, she had to come right out and ask him, "So what do you think?"

"When you say it should be someone who has seen you, what do you mean by 'seen'? Seen in what way?"

She just sat there for a second. "What does that mean?" she demanded. "How many ways are there to see? You look, you see."

"Well, yes," he said, firmly gripping his now empty water glass and shoving it back and forth on the table. "But take me, for example. I've seen you a lot, through the camera lens. Do I count?"

Mabel rolled her eyes. "Of course you don't count. You're in on it. You already know what I'm trying to do. You can't give an honest reaction. Like, *duh.*"

"So I'm not eligible?" he asked with what sounded an awful lot like relief.

"Of course not." Mabel had no idea why he was belaboring this. Just to be contrary, probably. "Don't worry—you are officially *not* on the roster of potential responders, okay?" Under her breath, she added, "As if I would put you on it, anyway."

"All right," he returned with a kind of snarly edge. "You don't have to push it. I've got it."

So first he was cranky that he might be on it, and then he was cranky he wasn't? She really had no clue how to deal with him.

"So," she said more sharply, picking up her pen and attacking the paper with it, "let's see who we've got, who is not and never was *you.*"

Frowning, she jotted down the names of a few possible men she knew who had never shown the least sign of being attracted to her.

"Phil Anderson, from the accounting department

at *Real Men,*" she mused. "Definitely a contender. He's very cute, I've met him several times when I picked up my checks at the magazine office, and he was friendly but not, you know, *friendly.*"

"Anderson? He's a jerk," Trace said so fast she barely had time to finish her last word.

She tapped her pen a few times, thinking it over. "Well, he did keep forgetting my name. He called me Marla once and Mary at least twice. And he left me hanging while he drooled over a couple of half-naked models." Mabel shrugged. "Given the women he sees every day, it seems unlikely he would give me a tumble even if I were... What was it you said? Even if I were naked on the Eisenhower Expressway at rush hour."

"Waiter!" Trace called out. "Could I have more water here, please? Plenty of ice."

"What is with you and the water?" she asked with some asperity.

"Thirsty," he said flatly.

As the waiter delivered Trace's water and the bottle of beer he'd ordered with his lunch, Mabel went back to her quest. "Okay, next choice. Brian O'Day. He was the guy I profiled for my part of the 'Chicago's Hottest Firefighters' piece. Very good-looking, if a little—"

This time he didn't wait for an opening. "He's a jerk, too."

"But you don't—"

"I read the profile you wrote. Sophia showed it to me." Trace set his jaw in a hard line. "The guy sounded to me like a first-class, A-1 pig. Arrogant, dumb as a bag of hammers, way too pumped up. Not your type."

Mabel blinked. "Sheesh! I was supposed to make him sound good. Was it that bad?"

"I read between the lines."

"I guess." She only had one more name to suggest. "Jerry Newberry. I liked him the best, anyway, and I don't think you'll find anything to object to. He's a commodities trader from the brokerage house one floor above the *Real Men* offices, and I've seen him— and more important, he's seen me—at The Hog & Heifer."

Trace raised an eyebrow at that one, stopping in mid-swig of his beer. "Do I dare ask what The Hog & Heifer is?"

"It's a dance club, right around the corner from *Real Men*." Not that she owed him an explanation. "I don't hang out there or anything, but I have met some people from *Real Men* there a few times for drinks. This Jerry Newberry was always there. Of course, he never noticed me, but isn't that the point?"

"Mabel, he sounds like a barfly. A sleazy, commodities trader barfly. This is not someone you should be—"

"He's also handsome and smart and funny—"

"A real paragon," Trace added grimly.

"Maybe." She lifted her chin, determined to get this one by him. What did he want her to do—go pick up some gnome under a bridge, and try her "hot" self out on *him?* "Listen, Trace, he fits the profile. I mean, he's seen me and didn't give me the time of day, plus he's attractive, relatively successful, and seems like a normal guy. If he goes for me in my remodeled state, then we'll know the fifty ways are responsible."

Trace leaned over the table, giving her the full benefit of those thick-lashed blue eyes. "Mabel," he said softly, sweetly, "I really don't think you need to—"

"Oh, yes, I do," she interrupted, staring down at the paper. Steeling herself, she penned in the number five, and carefully added her next item.

Walk on wild side at Hog & Heifer. Intended victim: Jerry N.

"Don't," Trace said quietly.

Mabel tuned him out. "So here's the plan—I put on the leather miniskirt with the halter top and saunter into The Hog & Heifer, and see if it catches Jerry's eye."

"Jerry's eye?" Trace sat back in his chair, his expression bleak. "I can promise you, it'll catch a lot more than his eye."

Mabel grinned. "Good. I've never done that before."

5

Tip #5: Buy lingerie, Kay.

There's nothing like something small and slinky to make a girl feel sinful from the inside out. It doesn't matter whether he even sees it—you'll know how sexy you are under there with every breath you take.

"IF YOU'RE GOING TO BE such a downer, I think I should do the lingerie by myself. Or maybe with some junior photographer. Someone else. A female."

"Mabel, we already went through this. I have to take the pictures," he said in a weary tone. "Believe me, if I could farm you out, I would."

Farm her out? He made her sound like Babe the Pig. She stormed ahead of him toward the Wispy-Wear Boutique's front door. "What did I do to you?"

"It's what you didn't do," he muttered.

"And what does that mean?"

She wanted to hit him with something hard. Really. The man was maddening! All he did was throw up roadblocks, send her brooding glances, and completely and totally mystify her. Her "undercover odyssey" was turning into a bad roller-coaster ride with Dr. Jekyll and Mr. Hyde's cuter brother.

"I need this job as much as you do," he said, which was interesting, if not even close to answering her question. "Let's just say I made a mess of things in my last position."

"Yeah," Mabel said dryly, turning back to him, searching his face for clues. "I heard."

"So I don't have a whole lot of leverage, here. Unless I want to be snapping photos for the *National Enquirer* from the back end of a speeding motorcycle, I had better make this *Real Men* gig work." His lips tilted into a grim smile. "I'm counting on you to make it work with me. Ready to sizzle, Mabel?"

"How about another day?" she tried. "We're both tired and cranky. Shouldn't we wait a day or two and come back to it rested and relaxed?"

He shook his head. "We have to do it now. Sophia's schedule puts us in a major time crunch, plus I'm borrowing darkroom space, and I have to develop this stuff and get it over to her like yesterday so she can see if it's going to work. Can't wait, Mabel."

Maybe he thought he would hustle her through the lingerie experience so fast that neither of them would notice this weird thing happening between them—whatever it was.

"We both know we have to do this," he told her, in a voice that made it clear going to a naughty undies boutique with her was akin to swallowing bad medicine. "We might as well just act like adults and get it over with. I'll stay on my side of the camera and you stay on yours, and we should be just fine."

"I'm perfectly capable of acting like an adult," she retorted. "In fact, that sounds dandy by me. Agreed? Adult, reasonable, professional? No idiotic jokes involving my name, no leering, no groping, no *nothing*."

Was that a twinkle in his eye? *How dare he enjoy this!* But all he said was, "Absolutely."

"Okay, then." She stood there, wishing she hadn't taken such a hard line, making it now incumbent upon her to march right in there and slap on some panties.

She figured Trace thought she was stalling again because she was scared. Goody Two Shoes Mabel, petrified and embarrassed by slutty stuff.

Au contraire. No, the WispyWear Boutique did not gross her out. Instead, it made her want to giggle.

She'd proposed that the two of them behave in an adult, reasonable, professional manner. Well, the WispyWear Boutique made her feel eager, excited, and a little *too* adult, as in Adults Only, Triple X, melting from the inside out.

Ludicrous, but true. Mabel Ivey, the girl who had never gone in for easy sex or cheap thrills, was only now discovering she had a "hot mama" hiding inside her, trying desperately to come out and play.

It was not the prospect of corsets or camisoles, but her reaction to them, that scared the pants off her. Which was a bad way of thinking about it, since she needed desperately to keep her pants *on*.

Your mission, whether you want to accept it or not, is to squash your "hot mama," she commanded herself.

One little lingerie store shouldn't be that intimidating. As she started to enter, she repeated the mantra. *I am strong, I am in control, I am...*

She was strong, she was in control, and she was staring at a red garter belt with little roses on the garters, attached to sheer scarlet stockings that looked like something you'd wear at a Bourbon Street bordello.

Mabel's mouth dropped open and she stopped halfway through the door, her eyes fixed on the display, her fingers pressed to the window. "Ohhh. That's adorable."

Once again, Trace was backing in, safeguarding his camera bag as he cleared the doorframe. Except he didn't clear the doorframe because Mabel was still in it. So, once again, he bumped into her from behind and knocked her off her pins.

But this time, he spun around quickly, hauling her up against him to keep her upright. There she was, dangling in midair, feeling the imprint of his hard, very male body from head to toe.

"Whew," she managed, exhaling all her air in one big whoosh.

"Are you all right?" His voice was low and a little husky. It was also right next to her ear, so close she could feel his warm breath tickle her hair.

Trace Cameron's fierce embrace, a garter belt with little roses, sheer red stockings, all wound together in a New Orleans bordello with red velvet curtains and a really big bed... Her imagination ran away with her so fast she could have written the novel, the screenplay *and* a sequel and had material to spare.

Oh, God. Was that all the longer her good intentions lasted? She was strong. She was in control.

She swallowed. "I think you'd better put me down now."

Trace held her a second longer than necessary. But then he let her go, sliding her down the front of him as he set her back on her own two feet. "Sorry. I guess if I'm going to hang around with you, I'm going to have to learn to proceed with caution through doorways.''

Mabel made a point of brushing herself off. ''If you weren't always in such a hurry, it wouldn't happen.''

''Somehow I didn't figure you'd be standing around gawking at a garter belt.''

''I wasn't...'' But she had been. ''Well,'' she continued lamely, ''I've never seen a red one. I'm not sure I've ever seen any garter belt, come to think of it, live and in person.''

''Oh, yeah?'' Trace smiled, and it had such a wicked tilt to it, it took her breath away. He leaned in over her, bracing an arm against the doorframe, blocking her path. Bending down very close, so close his lips were only an inch from hers, he whispered, ''I have.''

''I'll just bet you have.'' If he bent down another tiny bit, his lips could meet hers. She already knew he would taste like heat and strength and...desire. Forbidden desire.

It was clear he didn't know how *not* to flirt. So much for his promises. He was already misbehaving, and they hadn't even hit the stupid store yet. She ducked under him and pushed open the door, reminding herself of her mission.

This wasn't just a lingerie store, it was an opportunity. She was supposed to get fodder for scintillating words and phrases, for a smashing article that would knock Sophia Weston's socks off. No bordello fantasies, and no innuendo battles with the likes of Bulldozer Boy.

Work. Think about work.

She already had an angle of sorts for her ''Wear a tight dress, Tess'' material; all about how she was distressed at first but then started to enjoy it. But what was she going to do with lingerie?

She chewed her lip, studying the displays of scanty panties and lacy bras, feeling a little overheated and very greedy already. Even if she never wore them, she wanted to own the red garter belt and the ice-pink satin camisole with matching tap pants and the demure white-lace demi-bra and bikini pants and even the black fishnets and the bustier....

Stop. Whether she wanted to own it or not, it was pretty scandalous stuff. And she had no intention of modeling it for Trace or anyone else.

"I don't think the readers of *Real Men* are ready for photos of this on me," she said defiantly.

"I'm game," Trace said quickly, lifting his camera. "Shimmy in and go for it."

"You're a guy. Guys will look at anything. But *Real Men* is a women's magazine." She shook her head. Was he still trying to tease her? He looked awfully...hungry. Or something. Man alive, she wished she could figure him out. He was such a puzzle, it made him positively tantalizing.

This verbal fencing, all the dangerous glances, the lean-in that could so easily have turned into a kiss—was it just to keep her off-kilter? And what about the lecture about needing the job and having to "sizzle"?

She was sure it had been a game at the beginning, when any attraction between the two of them was coming from one direction—hers. But now, she wasn't sure of anything.

Except that he was one great-looking guy.

Like she wasn't in good company on that conclusion. All the women he photographed fell for him—wasn't that what Sophia had said? So no doubt they all wasted time gazing at him like lunkheads, wondering what the love god was thinking.

"Not me," Mabel said out loud. "I have a job to do."

"And I thought you just said you weren't going to do it."

"Because I won't parade around in my undies? Hardly." Mabel held up a pair of panties so skimpy they were barely a ribbon and a dime's worth of satin. Acidly, she announced, "No one, not even my mother, needs to see me in these."

Trace whipped out his camera and shot her waving the panties. It all happened so fast she didn't even have time to drop her mouth open in surprise.

"What are you doing?"

"You should've seen your expression. I told you, I don't pass up great shots." He shrugged. "So maybe you're right. We already did the budding sex kitten thing at Kuku. Maybe this time we're better off with fear and loathing on the lingerie trail."

"Fine by me." Making a face, Mabel gingerly dangled a leopard-print underwire bra from one hand, and the matching thong from the other. "Eeeeuw."

It was only after he'd snapped the picture that she surreptitiously examined the backside of the thong. "Who in her right mind would willingly wear this stuff?"

Click. He caught the look of disbelief. "Perfect," he told her.

"It's not my fault," she persisted. "That's got to feel awful. I mean, do you know where that goes?"

He made a little gasping noise, and she couldn't tell if he was trying not to laugh or just choking. "Yes, Mabel, I know where it goes." He shrugged, all innocence, his eyes wide and blue. "So why don't you try it on and find out? Isn't that your assignment?"

"Some things you can tell without trying." Dumping the animal prints back onto their table, she looked for something else to illustrate the "fear and loathing" he'd talked about. It wasn't hard. "Good grief, did you see this?"

She held up a witchy corset for him to see. It was a shiny, black vinyl thing, heavily boned, with long, lethal-looking laces up the back. "Just right for Scarlett O'Hara in a dominatrix phase," she remarked, giving it the once-over, sucking in her breath and absently hooking it on over her shirt just to see whether it would fit. Feeling quite absurd, she managed a cheesy smile and a silly pose for him to take her picture. It hurt to talk, but she did it, anyway. "This thing fits like an iron lung. Do you suppose it comes with its own whip?"

"You might like that. Trace's Tip #3: Get whipped in the stable, Mabel," he said with a sly smile. "Leather, whips, saddles. Hey, listen, if you want to horse around a little bit, I'll be happy to find a stable to shoot the pictures in. The proper background and all that."

Letting out a big sigh of disgust—or maybe just relief that she could get oxygen again—she unhooked the horrid corset and dropped it back onto the table. "I'm stable enough, thanks," she said sweetly. "It's you I'm worried about."

She debated whether she should remind him that he'd promised to inflict no more of those stupid rhymes on her. What did it really matter? He was just as infuriating, with or without his attempts at Mabel

quips. *Sable, cable, stable...* He had to run out of
rhymes sooner or later.

With Trace lagging behind, she wandered over to
a display of red items. Her gaze snagged on another
one of those rosy little garter belts and the matching
stockings, plus a whole bunch of other things some
enterprising designer had created to match. There was
even a teddy, with little roses scattered on the straps
and down the bodice.

Mabel stopped dead. "Oooh," she murmured, fin-
gering a long, slinky, red robe in one hand, clutching
that wonderful teddy in the other. "I think I need
this."

"You *need* it?" His voice dropped. "I can't help
it—I have to know what for."

"Just for... I don't know. For fun." Regretfully,
Mabel put aside the red collection and moved on.

"Oh, go on," Trace encouraged. "If you like it so
much, try it on. I've got enough of the humor angle,
with you looking disgusted. So why don't you model
some of that?"

Against her better judgment, Mabel actually considered it. After all, if it looked hideous, she didn't
have to come out of the dressing room.

And even if she did like it, she didn't have to show
him. She could try it on for herself, because she liked
it, not because it was part of her makeover.

"Jump at the chance, Nance." Those were her instructions, right? She could have this lovely lingerie,
and *Real Men* would pay for it....

"If it makes you uncomfortable, it's probably exactly what you should do," Trace said reasonably, but
there was something in his expression that reminded

her to beware of serpents offering apples. "Isn't that the whole point of this exercise?"

"The S&M corset makes me uncomfortable. This makes me…" Mabel paused. "Covetous."

"So? Doesn't that belong in your article?"

"Maybe." Without giving herself time to think it over properly, Mabel grabbed the teddy. At the last minute, her heart thumping, she spun around to a different table and snatched up a pair of black fishnets and matching garter belt, slip, and the long black robe. Every woman needed to try a garter belt once in her life, didn't she?

"The fifty tips specifically mention garter belt and fishnets, so I thought I'd better," she rushed to explain.

Behind her, Trace didn't say a word.

Mabel blocked him from her mind, thanking her lucky stars the fingernails were already gone and, this time, she could shed her own clothes and slip into the new things without his help. It would be much easier. Much less dangerous.

She tried the black-lace set first. The slip wasn't too bad, and the garter belt had a certain naughty energy, hidden underneath, but the fishnets…

They were just too silly.

Laughing out loud, she slipped the robe on over her shoulders to cover up the worst part of the view, and then gave herself the once-over in the mirror. "I'm sorry," she called out to Trace, "but you absolutely have to take a picture of this. American women deserve to know they should stay away from these horrible things. My thighs look like something Captain Ahab just harpooned."

"Bring it on out here," Trace responded.

"I'm supposed to be luring men, not getting them to take chastity vows," she said out loud, wondering where her notebook had gotten to and whether she ought to write that down.

Giggling, she made an entrance through the curtains of the tiny room, and then did a little turn. Dutifully, without a hint of enthusiasm, he clicked one photo.

"Oh, come on. If I can have a sense of humor about it, so can you," she told him.

But Trace wasn't laughing.

Maybe it was worse than she thought. Mabel scooted back into the dressing room, glancing at the mirror. No, she was right the first time. She looked idiotic. Oh, well. Maybe he was getting tired. Or maybe he didn't want to embarrass her by hooting too loudly.

She slid on the red teddy next, but it had thin spaghetti straps that formed an X in the back, and it took a minute to figure out how to get into it.

"Nasty," she said doubtfully, giving herself a good look in the glass. It was tight in the front, but the back gapped in a weird way. Meanwhile, the bottom was floppy in the front and stretched taut behind.

How disappointing. She'd fallen in love with it on the hanger. Even if the fishnets were dopey, she'd had high hopes for the red teddy.

"This one is even worse," she said indignantly, shoving out through the curtains and showing it off. "I think women should know just how terrible this whole lingerie thing is. It's like false advertising."

This time he did laugh. "Mabel, you have it on backward."

"I do not!"

"Yes, you do." Setting his camera aside, he turned her around and took her by the shoulders. "Hold still. Let's pull the straps over your head. Duck. Okay. There."

"But now the crisscross is in the front," she protested. "That can't be right."

"It isn't. I told you, you have it on backward." He stepped back and examined her. "But at least now the cross goes with the back of the dress, even if it's on your front."

Mabel looked down to the X on her chest, and then glanced back at the rear view. Damn the man. He was right. It *was* backward. "It's not a dress. But I hate it when you're right."

Trace was positively grinning as he raised his camera and reeled off a few shots.

"Hey! Why'd you do that?"

"Great picture," he returned, focusing from a different angle. "Unique, like you. And in one small photo, we've defined the hazards of lingerie. Now throw your hands up at your sides, palms up, like you're saying 'Oops.'"

"*That,* I can do. And you know what? It doesn't bother me in the least. Because I make a lot of mistakes, but I fix 'em, too. And that, as Sophia would say, is empowerment." She lifted her shoulders, put up her hands as ordered, and smiled big for the camera. "Oops!"

"Perfect." He relaxed, dropping the camera momentarily. "Okay, let's put it back the way it was so you can get out without choking yourself."

But as he reached for her, Mabel backed up. "I'm okay," she said, chin down, tugging at the first of the thin cords that formed the X, trying to get her head under it. "I can do it myself."

"I know you. You'll strangle yourself."

"No, I won't."

"Come on, Mabel. Don't be stubborn." He advanced, grabbing the fabric at the same moment she did.

Rrrrip. The strap split from its bodice, and two tiny rosebuds from the trim popped off and hit him in the chin.

"Oops," Mabel said out loud. She couldn't help it. The whole thing was so ridiculous, what with the backward teddy and the rosebud artillery.

She laughed, making a funny little whoop that sounded almost like a hiccup.

But Trace's hand was still clasped firmly on her bodice. And he wasn't laughing.

Yanking her close, Trace bent down and covered her lips with his. Greedy, relentless, hot, hard, his mouth possessed hers so fast she couldn't even resist, just hung on for dear life.

She was surprised, caught off guard. But that didn't mean she didn't respond. Oh, no. She kissed him back like she'd wanted to from the first minute she saw him.

It was fabulous.

She'd never been kissed like that—not even close. Her head was spinning, and she couldn't breathe, couldn't think. Not that she really wanted to.

She heard a hungry little moan as she wrapped her arms around his neck and pressed up into his embrace. Uh-oh. The moan came from *her.*

"Mabel," he murmured, brushing his lips over her cheek and her neck. "You are so sweet. So special."

Special? She really wished the thought hadn't popped into her head. But then again, thank goodness that it had. Of course he was a wonderful kisser; he'd had lots of practice.

"Is that what you say to all of them?" she asked, going still in his arms.

He lifted his head. "What?"

"All the women you photograph. All the ones who fall in love with you. Are they all special? Or is that just me?"

Trace stared down at her, his eyes a stormy shade of blue. "That's just some nonsense Sophia threw at you, and you bought it. All the women I photograph do not fall in love with me."

Mabel pushed away completely. It was hard to be self-righteous and dignified wearing a torn red teddy, but she did her best. "Oh, so it's only half of them?"

"No, of course not." He swore under his breath, glared at her, and turned away. "Okay, maybe half. Or they think they do. But it's not my fault," he added. "It's like falling for your doctor or your shrink. Transference, isn't that what they call it? I don't encourage it. And I don't kiss them."

"Well, aren't I lucky?" she mocked. "I got kissed. Let's see—I must be in group B, the ones who don't fall under your spell right off the bat." She chose to ignore the fact that she had, in fact, fallen under his spell from the word go. A technicality. And as long as he didn't know, it didn't count. "I suppose when you hit a challenge, you have to keep trying. You charm my cat, you ogle my..." She tried to think of a decent word. "You ogle my behind, you make up sexy jokes about my name, about naked in sable and porn on cable and whips in the stable—" she was really getting rolling now ''—and then when I still don't succumb, you kiss me. Out of the blue. For nothing.''

"The last thing I wanted to do was make you *succumb*,'' he argued, giving that last word a really dirty spin. "I've tried ignoring you. I've tried teasing you just to make you so mad you'll stay away from *me*. I was even mean on purpose. It didn't matter.''

Mabel backed off, trying to take this in. He seemed angry enough that she thought he might actually be telling the truth. Could this be true? This passion for *her?* Whoa. Where was her notepad when she needed it? She had to sort this through. When, exactly, had this happened?

He sighed, running a hasty hand through his hair. "It just doesn't matter. No matter what I do, I keep sliding back into wanting you. And I am not the kind of guy who looks the other way when something like this bites me on the butt, no matter how stupid I know it is, no matter how much I don't want it, no matter how many vows I take.''

How stupid it was? How much he didn't want it? "Oh, that's lovely! Well, don't worry, Mr. Love God Photo King—''

"'Love God Photo King'?'' he interrupted. "What is that supposed to mean?''

"It's an insult,'' she retorted. Not a really quality insult, but she was doing her best on the spur of the moment. "Anyway, Mr. Whoever-You-Are, you don't have to worry, because I will not be biting you on the butt anymore.'' She stopped, horrified. "I didn't mean—''

"I know what you meant.''

"Good.'' Mabel lifted her chin and gave him a

glacial stare. She finally thought she had a bead on this, and it wasn't pretty.

When he looked at Mabel he saw nothing he wanted, but a certain other part of his anatomy was egging him on. And it was a part he'd had very little practice denying.

Trace was a serial seducer.

He couldn't help himself. He liked women, and he liked making love to them, with or without his camera. So now, even though he was trying to stop, his habit of seduction was just too hard to break.

Well, Mabel Ivey was no man's *habit*. "I know perfectly well that this is just a game for you. Confuse and conquer. But I don't play games like that."

"This is no game." And then he grabbed her and kissed her again.

Oh, God. How could it feel so good when it was so very wrong? Mabel was sinking fast, tasting his lips, simmering in his heat, uncoiling with desire like it was a ball of Polly's yarn.

But Trace pulled away this time.

"Sorry," he whispered. "You just make me so damn mad. And yet you make me laugh at the same time. I admit it—I don't get you, Mabel."

She was a little wobbly. Damn him for turning her on and off like a toaster! "Nobody's asking you to get me," she mumbled, wiping her lips.

"But I like you," he persisted, taking her by the shoulders, gazing deep into her eyes. "That's why I'm trying to be noble, though Lord knows, it's not my strong suit. But I don't want to pull you into something that neither of us thinks is a good idea." His expression was rueful, his eyes searching. "What are we going to do about this, Mabel?"

"Not a darn thing," she said darkly, shaking off his hands. "It's stupid, it makes no sense, and we have a job to do. Look, I'm sure we're both just influenced by all this...lingerie. Away from here, we'll be fine," she finished weakly.

Trace's lips curved into a very dubious smile. "Sure, we will."

"Today is Tuesday," Mabel went on, speaking more forcefully. "I know we're under the gun, time-wise, but we can afford a forty-eight-hour breather. It'll give you a chance to hit the darkroom with what we have so far, and I can..." She smiled firmly. "I can get ready for my walk on the wild side at The Hog & Heifer. Thursday is the best night for that, anyway."

"A forty-eight-hour breather, huh?" he asked softly.

"Exactly." Mabel wheeled away, very ready to be out of this blasted teddy and headed for home, where she could jump into sweats, have a cup of tea, and cuddle her kitty. "So we'll do our little spin into sin with you on one side of The Hog & Heifer and me on the other, and we'll be just fine."

"Spin into sin?" he echoed, laughing. "Mabel, where do you get this stuff?"

"I don't know. It's just there." She wished he would stop confusing her. The way he'd stopped in mid-argument to admire her way with words bewildered her all over again. "We're agreed, then? We'll meet at The Hog & Heifer at eight sharp, Thursday night." She marched away from him, repeating her words like a mantra, even if she was way too shaky to be sure she believed herself. "And we'll be just fine."

Behind her, she could have sworn she heard him whisper it, too.

"Just fine."

Who exactly were they kidding?

6

Tip #26: Dance until dawn, Fawn.

Remember those swoony old Fred-and-Ginger movies, where they went cheek to cheek and found love and romance? Remember your high-school prom, where they had to pry boys and girls apart with rulers to keep them from wanton acts right there on the dance floor? Dancing can be like rubbing two sticks together, except it's two warm, willing bodies. Watch out for sparks!

AT PRECISELY SIX-THIRTY, Mabel rose from her bath, smelling of Temptress soap, raring to do battle.

Calm, with just a tiny tremor of nerves, she began to don the outfit she had so carefully laid out on her bed—and even more carefully kept away from Polly's claws. First, she slipped into the black-lace panties purchased at the WispyWear Boutique, plus a pair of sheer panty hose from the regular old drugstore. She might be on an expense account, but she was no idiot.

On her trip to the corner store, she'd also picked up new, less dangerous fingernails—this time with a handy removal kit—a replacement blow-dryer, a couple of rub-on tattoos, and even a fake navel ring. And then she'd spent the rest of her day chasing down leather clothes to complete her outfit.

Now, scanning her silhouette in the mirror, Mabel fastened on the leather halter top, wiggling to get it to fit right, and then slid into the matching miniskirt.

So far, so good. Or at least as long as she left her contacts out, so that there was this lovely unfocused fog around her reflection.

There was a gap of a good three inches between the halter and the skirt, and Mabel decorated the gap with a press-on rose tattoo on one side of her middle, and the clip-on ring for her navel. The rose was a little crooked, but the only way someone could tell was if he had his face pressed up against her stomach. How likely was that?

She rubbed the other tattoo—a dolphin—onto her shoulder, and spent a moment or two regretting that she wasn't brave enough to dye her hair either jet-black or peroxide blond for the total Biker Chick look. But once it was slicked back with gel and teased up according to Jean-Paul's instructions, it would have to do.

Then Mabel slathered on the makeup, frowning as she referred to her handy notebook for specific diagrams and notes.

"Aha!" she cried, beaming at the thick, black streaks of eyeliner, which only wobbled a little in one corner. If she piled on the mascara, no one would even notice.

This was kind of like being in the school play! If the play was either *Grease* or *Caged Vixens*.

Feeling friskier by the minute, Mabel slung a stark black leather jacket around her shoulders—one with all kinds of zippers, just like Trace had recommended—and, for the pièce de résistance, slid her legs into new, very tall boots. Thigh-high boots hadn't been easy to find, and the clientele at the place she'd gotten them had been pretty scary, but she had them now, and they were looking *fine*.

"Biker chicks of the world, unite!" she declared, squinting at her mirror image. "The Hog & Heifer isn't going to know what hit it."

And neither would Trace Cameron.

"Mabel, Mabel, Mabel," she chastised herself quickly. "Forget about him. Tonight you're targeting Jerry Newberry, commodities broker. For all you know, he's every bit the jerk, every bit the playboy, as Trace. But for tonight, Jerry is your prey."

Giving herself one last, hazy go-over, she yanked her halter top back to where it belonged, growled at her hazy reflection for courage, and sauntered out of the apartment.

It was amazing how quickly she caught a cab. Plus, two others came screaming over to her side of the street at the same time, all vying for the privilege of driving her. This was weird.

She'd stowed her pad and pen in the big, ugly bag she was carrying, along with her glasses—just for an emergency—a ton of makeup, haircare products, and the usual money and ID. She was discovering just how much work—and upkeep—it took to look this trashy. Surreptitiously, she pulled out her notebook and hastily wrote down her newest discovery.

Bonus: Dress like a hot babe, and taxis will screech to a stop to pick you up.

Mabel told the cabbie to pull over at the corner nearest to The Hog & Heifer, about a half block away.

Her first challenge was to ease herself out of the car in the tight leather skirt without flashing half her bottom or most of her thighs at the city of Chicago. She was already starting to sweat by the time her booted feet hit the cement, and she heard a long wolf whistle and a few hoots and hollers. Well, at least she stayed upright this time.

Once out, she tried to remember to stride right along and act like she always looked this way. But mentally, she was making practical notes for the benefit of her future article, one about being sure you could get up and down in your skirt, and another about the torrid temperature of leather right next to your skin.

Yikes! Almost losing a heel to a sidewalk grate brought her back to reality. Then she noticed that some guy had stopped in the middle of the sidewalk to stare at her back view, while another was trying to get in front of her, waving and smirking. A third was hovering in her vicinity, inclining his head like he wanted to direct her over to some dark doorway. All within the space of a half block!

Now, if she only knew how to deal with all the attention. If this had happened a week ago, she would have sworn they were kidding. But they didn't look like this was a joke. Right there on the sidewalk, Mabel added a few notes to her "undercover odyssey" journal.

Leather outfit definitely attracting all comers— three within half block, plus wolf whistles getting out of cab.

Now that she believed strange men could be drawn to her just because of the way she was dressed, what did she do about it?

I'll just ignore it, she decided. It wasn't part of the plan to strike up conversations with guys on the street—especially losers like that bunch.

As she walked along, she found herself swept up in a major observation that she knew she would never share with the readers of *Real Men*. *It's one thing to strike a few sparks with Trace Cameron, but quite another to have sleazebuckets hooting at you on the street.*

Mabel soldiered on to The Hog & Heifer, her admirers trailing behind. She felt like whoever that guy was who lured all the rats out of town. The Pied Piper, that was it. Only she was The Pied Hussy.

It was a relief to swing open the door of the club, to leave the creeps out on the street. Gazing around, Mabel took in the out-of-focus panorama of after-work drinkers and dancers, all busy with their own affairs, unimpressed by a lone woman even if she was tarted up in leather. The place was packed, and it was hopping.

Hmm. She squinted into the dimness, but she didn't see Trace.

"He'd better be here," she muttered. "I can't photograph my 'undercover odyssey' myself."

She didn't know how she felt about seeing him again, after the weirdness of their last encounter. But she couldn't deny that fluttery anticipation in the pit of her stomach.

"Looking for me?" he asked, raising his voice over the music. Emerging from the smoke and confusion, he carried his ever-present camera bag over his shoulder and a long-necked beer in one hand. And he looked fabulous.

The flutters increased to something in the neighborhood of drumbeats.

"Are you supposed to be drinking on the job?" Mabel inquired, just as the music dropped, which made her question sound a lot louder than she'd anticipated.

Trace grinned, which surprised her. "You know, Mabel, even with your nose in the air, it's hard to take you seriously when you're dressed like that. Nice outfit, by the way. I guess I can tell what you did with your forty-eight hours off. Stalked and tanned a few black cows, did you?"

She'd forgotten for a moment that she *was* dressed like that. Trying not to fidget under his scrutiny, she reminded him, "The boots were your idea. I'm just following your Biker Chick profile, you know. So if I look ridiculous, it's your fault."

"Did I say you looked ridiculous?"

No, but I saw the twinkle in your damn blue eyes. She guessed that answered the question of what effect her outfit would have on him. Her fingers itched to get that down in black-and-white: that icky men might be whistling, but MIQ was chuckling. So she was right. The looks, the kisses...they were just a game to him. A game he'd now abandoned as he apparently moved on to the next seduction in the series.

He'd regained his senses. Even if she hadn't.

As he took another swig from the brown bottle, she demanded, "Can you still focus if you're tanked up on that stuff?"

"I'm not tanked in the least, and yes," he said

wryly, "I can focus just fine." He gave her a skeptical look up and down. "Your rose is crooked."

"My...?"

"Rose. The one tattooed on your tummy."

What did he have, X-ray vision? In a dark, smoky bar, with her jacket and shoulder bag obscuring his view, how in blazes did he notice that her tattoo was a little tipped? "How can you...? Oh, never mind." The music started again, an old song about honky-tonk women, and Mabel took it as her cue. "Do you see Jerry Newberry anywhere? You know, my prey."

He laughed. "Your 'prey'? I thought this was a walk on the wild side, not a psycho-thriller."

"Whatever." As unobtrusively as she could manage, she slipped her glasses out of her bag and lifted them up to her nose, peering through the lenses. "There he is, over at the bar."

Her "prey" was surrounded by a cluster of well-dressed men and women, all talking, gesturing, knocking back cocktails. Jerry looked pretty much the way she remembered him: medium height, medium build, with light hair and pale eyes. He was attractive enough, she supposed, if a bit sloshy after he'd chugged down whatever was in the empty glasses piled in front of him. Of course, with Trace in the same place, it was hard for anybody else to look that great. Now, Jerry's nose seemed a little stubby, his lips a tad thin. And his chin—well, it was positively weak.

But for her purposes, Jerry was perfect. And the fact that there were several women already with him made it even better. If she snared him under these circumstances, it would prove the whole luring-a-lover thesis.

Slipping her glasses back into her bag, she announced, "I'm going in. You just keep shooting, Photo Boy."

"I thought I was Love God Photo King."

"You've been demoted."

Behind her, Trace laughed again, dragging out his camera to record her foray. *Damn his hide.* He hadn't gotten any better in the forty-eight-hour respite. No better at all.

Mabel stopped, turned, and gave him her best attempt at a Biker Chick snarl. She was gratified when he raised the camera and snapped the pose, but not so happy to see him snickering behind the lens.

Forcibly putting him out of her mind, Mabel sidled through the tables, dodging the edge of the dance floor, giving stern looks and sterner words to the guys who tried to pursue her along the way. Good grief. This siren stuff was exhausting.

Luckily, Jerry was soon within striking range. Occupied with his own crowd, he didn't notice Mabel as she advanced from the rear. So she posed artfully on the stool behind him, rolled around a little nearer, and breathed in his ear.

"Buy me a drink?" she whispered, just the way they did it in the movies.

"Huh?" He spun around, clearly irritated. "Who are…?"

But then she crossed her legs, smiled brazenly, and gave him a good look at her Biker Chick charms.

Drool practically dripped on his chin. His eyes remained riveted to her modest cleavage, which looked more impressive than it really was in the V of the leather halter.

Mabel broke character long enough to glance

around, searching for Trace somewhere in the shadows. If he didn't get a shot of the half-witted look on Jerry Newberry's face, she was going to kill him.

"H-huh?" Jerry mumbled, finally lifting his gaze far enough to find out she had a face. "What did you say?"

"I asked if you were going to buy me a drink," she said with a definite edge. Forget the wispy voice; she was going to have to spell things out for this goon. Show him a little leather, and his IQ dropped one hundred points.

"Yeah. Drink. Sure. Barkeep, the lady's thirsty." He turned to her, his eyes glazed and hopeful. "What will you have?"

Oh, heavens. What did she do now? The list of tips didn't tell her what to order. She didn't suppose a glass of water would go with the outfit. But it was so hot and steamy under all that leather—she might as well be living inside a handbag—and plain old water was what she really wanted.

"Scotch and water," she improvised, wiping a sleeve across her brow, hoping she hadn't accidentally smeared any of her makeup. "In separate glasses."

Jerry was either too drunk or too besotted to care, although the bartender gave her a weird look. Still, she drank the water, pretended to sip the Scotch, and then said loudly, "Fill me up again," tapping the water glass.

"I think I'm in love," Jerry mumbled, leaning on his elbow and offering a goofy grin. "Where'd you come from, beautiful lady?"

Oh, pu-leez. "I came from the other side of the bar," she returned.

"Huh?"

"Nothing." Meanwhile, she was melting. Her outfit was impossible. Giving in, she shrugged out of the suffocating jacket, baring her shoulders, her dolphin tattoo, and most of her back to Jerry's avid gaze.

"You are so hot," the guy rasped, shoving his stool even closer.

"Yes, I know." She felt about a hundred and twenty degrees, even without the motorcycle jacket. Chewing her lip and undoubtedly marring the gloss of her dark plum lipstick, Mabel cast her glance one way and then the other. Where was Trace? She didn't dare fetch her glasses one more time to look for him. Could she assume he was getting this on film?

Because if he wasn't taking pictures, she wasn't participating in this overheated farce for one more minute.

"Barkeep, set 'er up again." Jerry slapped a twenty down on the bar. Then he nudged Mabel with his elbow, almost knocking her off her stool. "Drink up, babe."

She took a tiny sip, letting the Scotch sit under her tongue long enough to anesthetize her bottom teeth, and quietly shoved the rest of the tumbler down the bar far enough to look like it belonged to someone else. Quickly, she swallowed half her water as a chaser.

"So, Jerry," she began, racking her brain for conversational gambits, "do you…come here often?"

"Yeah. Love The Hog & Heifer. Love it. Especially Thursdays." He chuckled, tossing back the rest of his martini and gulping down the olive. "Let's dance, huh?"

"Dance?"

But she didn't have a choice. Although she tried to grab for the bar as an anchor, Jerry was already dragging her out onto the dance floor. Neither her tight leather skirt nor her high-heeled boots made dancing easy, but it was some silly disco tune about loving the nightlife, so she just shuffled her feet a little and tried to stay away from Jerry's graspy paws.

It wasn't easy. Even though the song didn't fit, he clasped her close and sort of rested his chin against her cheek, one hand firmly on her leather-clad bottom, and the other tickling her bare midriff. He smelled like liquor, his bleary comments were gross, and Mabel quickly decided this "hot" life wasn't all it was cracked up to be.

When Jerry tried to kiss her, right there in front of all the other dancers, she stretched away far enough to need a chiropractor.

"I can't keep my hands off you, baby," Jerry told her, as if it were a compliment.

"Yeah, I noticed." She pushed him back, but he had her in a vise grip. "Give it a rest, will you?"

"Come on, babe," he tried. "You know you like it."

"No," she said plainly. "I don't."

But then Trace and his camera came into view just over Jerry's shoulder. She smiled, trying to make it look as though she were enjoying herself, even though she felt like the world's biggest goon.

From this distance, she could tell Trace was glowering at her. Too dark or too bad an angle for good pictures? Well, that was his problem.

But if Trace was cranky, Jerry was having a great time. Completely without warning, he yanked her into a wild spin that nearly sent her into the rafters. "Yeesh," she cried. "What was that?"

"Slick, huh?" Jerry crowed. "I've been taking lessons."

Mabel thought "sick" was closer than "slick," but she kept her mouth shut. All she could do was hang on and try not to fall down as Jerry threw his dancing-fool moves.

And then the disco beat stopped in mid-song. *Phew,* she thought, ready to sit down. She took a step in that direction.

"Attention, everyone!" a chirpy woman said, dragging a microphone onto the edge of the floor. "It's nine o'clock, and you know what that means."

Mabel didn't have a clue. But Jerry whooped, "Yeah! Swing lessons!"

"Sw-wing lessons?"

"Thursday is Hog & Heifer Swing Night!" the woman declared happily. "Swing is the hottest dance around, and we know you all love learning the new moves. We're going to assume you've got the basic heel-toe-backstep-down, and move on to the Pretzel, the Fender Bend, and the Hip-Knotic. Everybody ready?"

Mabel wasn't. But once again Jerry didn't give her a choice. As soon as the music started—something that sounded like it came from an old Bette Midler record—Jerry snaked a sweaty arm around her waist, reeled her in close, and began some hippity-hoppety dance that bore no relation to anything she'd ever experienced in her life.

"Okay, slide together, slide together, behind the back, spin her out, boys, and rock back!" cried the woman who was supposed to be leading this lesson.

But Jerry's feet weren't following instructions, and Mabel had lost any semblance of her Biker Chick persona. A real tough girl would have kneed him in the groin and walked out of there at the first sign of swing lessons. Mabel just tried to keep from getting squeezed to death or trampled.

The things she did in search of a good job and a decent paycheck.

How was it possible for Jerry to be stuck like glue to her midsection, while his feet were tromping all over hers? She was going to be black-and-blue before this thing was over.

"Oof," she managed, as he swung her out wildly, sending her skidding within inches of the microphone stand. The instructor lady plucked the mike out of the way just in time to prevent a collision.

"We're doing great!" Jerry shouted, hauling her back against his chest, flinging her this way and that as if she were a rag doll. "We don't need no stinking lessons!"

"Aieee!" she cried, as her boot clipped a poor boy who was trying to hoist his girlfriend over his head.

Whir. Click. The telltale signs that Trace was close by.

"We must look fantastic together," her dancing partner said with glee. "Some guy is taking a million pictures."

Mabel didn't think pictures of her at this moment were what *Real Men* women were looking for. Her toes hurt, her skirt was riding up, and perspiration was slithering down inside her halter top. She just wanted to go home, take a shower to wash off the gunk and sweat, and collapse in her own bed. Solo.

Instead, she was stuck fending off Mr. Grabby and

his two left feet. "Can we sit down?" she shouted, purposely angling around so that Trace and his camera were blocked from recording her flushed, wilted face.

"Thirsty?" Jerry yelled back. "Or maybe you wanna leave, huh? If you're in a hurry, there are plenty of dark corners. A little makeout with old Jer might be just what you need, sweet thing."

And then he tried to wink at her, but only got out a sloppy leer.

She got the idea. "No, I just want to sit down."

Okay, so she sounded whiny and not at all seductive. Jerry didn't seem to mind. Dark corners? With him? *Bleah.*

Trace, on the other hand, looked positively grim as she and Jerry exited the dance floor in front of him.

"How about a dance?" he asked, catching her arm. His eyes were moody and his jaw was clenched in a hard line.

"I can't," she whispered. "As you very well know. Because I'm... I'm undercover."

"What you are is skating on thin ice," he hissed.

"Hey, pal, she's with me," Jerry said angrily, jabbing a finger in Trace's face. "You just take your pictures and leave her alone."

"Chill out," Trace commanded, in a voice that brooked no objections. But he stepped back and let the two of them pass.

Mabel almost wished that he hadn't, although a fistfight between her photographer and her intended victim wouldn't really fit into the "ho-hum-to-hot" article she intended. This evening—this "walk on the wild side"—was supposed to be fun and exciting, a chance for her to attract a man and then lead him around by the nose.

Instead she got this sloppy grabfest with Jerry Newberry. If she let the boys scuffle, putting herself into dopey damsel-in-distress territory, things would be even worse.

Back on her barstool, she sighed, casting a glance around at Trace. Maybe she should have taken her opportunity to dump Jerry and hide behind Trace. She didn't know what she hoped to accomplish at this point, anyway. Her thesis—that Jerry would notice her now in a way he never had before—was long since proved.

And surely Trace had enough photos to accompany whatever text she wrote about this evening in the Bizarro World.

"Honey, sweetie," Mr. Bizarre himself cooed, handing her the untouched glass of Scotch. "Bombs away. We'll have a couple more drinks, and then..." He bent over far enough to drop a wet kiss on her bare shoulder. His voice was husky and insistent, and he was straddling his stool in a way that pretty much trapped her. "Then we'll go back to my place. Or wherever. Those dark corners are starting to look pretty good to me."

"Um, well... Not to me."

"You don't see a girl like you every day," he went on, sliding aside her hair to try to kiss her on the neck. "I can tell you are one wild lady."

Mabel moved back just in time, slapping a hand over the nape of her neck to keep his lips away. "Stop that."

"In that leather getup, you, lady, are too hot to handle."

"Not really," she said politely, twisting the other way. And she'd thought dancing was dangerous. Now she was sweaty, grumpy *and* claustrophobic. How did she get out of this?

The "50 Ways to Lure a Lover" list clearly needed an addendum. Just a couple of ways to get rid of one would have been very handy at that moment.

"Um, I know," she decided, trying to rise from her barstool with Jerry draped all over her. "We've rested. Time to get back out on that dance floor."

"Oh, yeah. I love to dance," Jerry responded, as she'd hoped he would. "It's like foreplay."

With him, it was like Greco-Roman wrestling. Accepting the lesser of these two evils, Mabel allowed herself to be led back into the arena.

"Are you sure you want to bring your drink with you?" she asked doubtfully, noticing the full glass of amber liquid in Jerry's free hand.

"It gets too hot out here." With a grimace, he took a healthy gulp. "This way I can dance and drink without wasting any time."

"Uh-huh." She stayed where she was, slightly out of reach, ready to bolt as soon as he strayed far enough. She had it all planned—she would spin away and never come back, accomplishing her exit all by herself, like a woman with her hands firmly on the reins of her own destiny. Let Trace snap *that!*

But Jerry started to get fussy. "What's the matter, babe? You backing off? You come on to me like gangbusters, you dress like that, like an advertisement, and *now* you're backing off?"

"My outfit isn't an advertisement," she returned. "It's just..."

She didn't suppose Jerry would understand if she

told him it was an experiment. It was supposed to have been so scientific, so neat, to waltz into The Hog & Heifer, to test her before-and-after personas, and then waltz right out again.

So why was everything such a mess?

She had to believe it was all Trace's fault. She didn't have a theory that supported that, but she would think of one, given time.

Jerry changed tactics, whispering, "C'mere, sweet thing," in a wheedling tone. He pressed his cool, wet glass into the small of her back, closing his eyes and jamming her up against him.

Yuck! "Hold on just a minute, there," Mabel protested, squirming out of his grasp, shoving him backward.

But Jerry stumbled. He reached for her to steady himself, and ended up dumping his whole drink on her.

As Mabel squealed, cold liquid and ice went shooting down inside her leather halter top. Horrified, in major distress, she caught a glimpse of Jerry's grin as he said, "Let me lick that off for you."

But he wasn't grinning for long.

Just as Mabel cried, "You, you *cretin*, you!" Trace jumped in from out of nowhere. He socked Jerry Newberry hard in the jaw, sending him reeling to the floor.

Mabel just sort of stood there, dripping, glancing back and forth between the two men—one in a messy heap on the floor and the other one snarling at her.

Before she had a chance to do more than sputter, Jerry mumbled something ugly and started to rise, and Trace swore out loudly.

"Don't you dare hit him," she managed. Even Mabel wasn't sure which one she was talking to.

It didn't matter. Before the words had even left her lips, Trace had bonked Jerry on the head one more time, grabbed her around the waist, and started to haul her out of there.

7

One way to spice up your ho-hum life is to take a little vacation from those same old haunts, the places where you see the same old faces, the same old MEN. Try somewhere you've never been, somewhere with a whole new attitude. Maybe, just maybe, you'll discover a whole new you.

TRACE WAS FURIOUS. He couldn't remember ever being this angry at a woman. Oh, sure, he'd been less than thrilled when Rita Devon had thrown half a plate of clams casino at him. But *she* was the one who'd been really mad. He'd just laughed.

"Put me down!" Mabel ordered, kicking her damn boots, wiggling in his grip, generally making his life miserable.

"No." He kept moving toward the door, as Hog & Heifer patrons parted like the Red Sea. Trace didn't care whether they gave him a clear path or not, or whether Mabel hollered bloody murder. He had every intention of carting her sorry behind out of there, no matter what she did.

"Put me down—I can't leave!"

Now that they had cleared the front door, he dropped her unceremoniously on the sidewalk.

"Mabel," he said, in the coldest voice he had in his arsenal, "if you tell me you were enjoying that, I really will dump you in the Chicago River. Put that in your story."

"Enjoying it? With Jerry, you mean? Heavens, no." She frowned at him, retreating a step. "But I have to go back."

"You can't," he said flatly. "Not dressed like that."

"I went in there dressed like this before."

Trace snapped, "You weren't *wet* before."

"Wet?" She glanced down at her front, where the leather now clung like a second skin. There were ice cubes down there, sending a chill right where it counted, giving her the perkiest nipples this side of *Playboy*.

Mabel blushed scarlet everywhere she had bare skin. And that was a lot of places.

"Oh, my God. I—I didn't notice." Hastily, she crossed her arms over her chest.

Yeah, well, he'd noticed a while ago. And so had her pal Jerry, who had offered to *lick* it off for her. Trace's lip curled.

"Let's get out of here, Mabel. Now. Before one or both of us gets arrested. My car's parked around the corner." He reached for her, but she shook her head.

"No. I can't." She kept one arm over her breasts, but held the other one out in front of her, warding him off. "One—I refuse to be manhandled, pushed or groped by any more men this evening. And that includes you. So keep your paws to yourself, buster."

"Fine time to start that rule," he muttered.

"Two," she continued, her voice rising. "If you would just listen to me for a minute, I would tell you that the reason I can't leave is *not* because I'm dying to go a couple more rounds with Jerry 'The Octopus' Newberry, but because I left my jacket and my bag at the bar. You know, when that imbecile dragged me to the dance floor." She was so agitated she was practically hopping. "That jacket was very expensive. And my glasses and my driver's license and even my notebook are in the bag! I can't go without them. I'm sure..." She hesitated, licking her lip. "I'm sure I can sneak back in there, grab my stuff, and get out really quickly without anyone noticing."

"You're sure, are you? In that outfit? You're kidding, right?"

"No, I'm not kidding." Her chin was trembling, but she held it high.

"Mabel, you're making me insane."

"I'll agree with the conclusion, although the cause is still up in the air."

He had no idea what that was supposed to mean, but coming from Mabel, it had to be an insult.

"Look," he said tersely. "You wait here. Stand near the door, keep your head down, and don't talk to anyone. Here." He took off his jacket and set it over her shoulders. "I mean it, Mabel. Keep your mouth shut. Oh, and hold this for me." He handed over his camera bag. No one ever touched that bag but him, but he knew he had to make an exception if he was going to go barreling into The Hog & Heifer like Indiana Jones. "I suppose if anyone accosts you, you can hit him with my Nikon. It's the heaviest."

Mabel studied the various compartments of the bag,

clearly intent on following instructions. "Which one am I supposed to hit him with?"

"I was joking."

"Oh." She shrugged into the jacket, pulling it across her front, looping the camera bag over that. "I could handle this myself, you know. I could go back in there."

But he could tell it was just a token protest. It was written all over her expressive face—she was relieved not to have to pluck her belongings from the tentacles of Jerry "The Octopus" Newberry. She was relieved to stay out of it.

"It's okay, Mabel," he said with a certain touch of irony. "You don't have to thank me. Just don't get into trouble while I'm gone."

As if that kind of warning would do any good where Mabel was concerned. For someone who was so determined to stay in control, she had a real knack for stirring things up.

Shaking his head, Trace left her alone on the sidewalk as he braved the hordes at The Hog & Heifer in search of her lost property.

As he pushed through the crowd to get to the bar, he promised himself he would never again set foot inside any place that had either the word *Hog* or *Heifer* in its name, no matter how many of Mabel's possessions were inside. Still, this was a relatively easy mission. He remembered exactly where she'd been sitting. Through his lens, he'd watched Mabel get slobbered on by that jerk long enough to have the specifics imprinted on his brain.

The only tricky part was eluding Jerry, who had to be loaded for bear by now, after losing his "lady" and getting knocked down twice. Trace kept an eye

out, but got lucky this time. The Octopus was nowhere to be seen—probably off slobbering on someone else. So Trace strolled in from the side, casually
snagged Mabel's gear, and quietly made for the exit
with all due speed.

And then, when he got back to her, he actually
grinned as he tossed her the bag and switched jackets.
Now that was weird. After successfully completing
his task, he felt like a...hero.

"Thank you," she rushed to say, clasping her huge
purse to her chest as if it were solid gold. "I really,
really appreciate this."

Trace shrugged. "'S okay."

He'd certainly never been anyone's idea of a hero
before. And yet, twice in one night, he'd leaped in
and rescued Mabel. Okay, so the second time—the
foray for her things—hadn't required much in the way
of heroics. But it could have. And the fisticuffs on
the dance floor had definitely been he-man stuff.

This was very unlike him. What was up with that?
He wasn't quite sure how he felt about turning over
a new leaf this late in his career.

But as he drove her home, he didn't get much
chance to mull it over. Mabel was gabbing away
about something, still talking a mile a minute as she
pulled out a notepad and began to scribble.

"It was so different from what I expected," she
told him, scooting around in her seat to face him better. "I mean, would you have thought that someone
like Jerry Newberry would turn out to be such a go-
rilla? I'm still shocked. Do you think that's always
what happens when you dress like a, well, like a slut-
puppy?"

"'Slut-puppy'? That's a new one."

"Okay, okay. A tart, a sleaze, a 'ho. I was trying for basic 'sexy,' but I guess maybe I went too far. Was it that, do you think?"

"Mabel, how would I know? I've never dressed like a slut-puppy, a tart, a sleaze *or* a 'ho," he returned, concentrating on the road in front of him.

"Yes, but you've seen women dressed like that. I mean, you've taken their pictures. I've seen them! In one magazine, you did a supermodel naked in a fishnet, and another one in three shells and some string. And then there was the cover with the girl wearing nothing but a few grains of sand."

"A real fan of my work, are you? Why, Mabel, I had no idea."

"I did my research—most of it yesterday. And you have to admit, you've seen lots of women in various states of undress. So you must have an opinion." She was really getting into this, waving her hands to emphasize her points. "So? Would you have expected Jerry to get all gropey like that? Do guys always behave that way in the face of trashy clothes? Which were very expensive, by the way, so why they're called trashy I don't know. Or—and this is what I think—it had nothing to do with me, and Jerry was a major creep from the word go, hiding behind this regular-cute-guy facade."

Trace paused, a bit taken aback by her torrent of words. Obviously, Mabel was running under the buzz of delayed adrenaline, her mouth just now catching up with the wild adventure she'd had.

"Well?" she prompted.

"Which question would you like me to answer first?" he asked dryly. While he was glad she hadn't ended up shell-shocked, he wasn't sure all this bubbly enthusiasm was a great idea, either.

"Oh. You can answer any of them."

"Fine." He gave her a jaded look. "I'll start at the beginning. Yes, I expected Jerry Newberry to act like a dog. I warned you, remember?"

"Well, yes, sort of. But you were being so grumpy, I just figured your objections were part of the general party-pooper thing."

"I've never been a party pooper in my life," Trace protested. "I told you he sounded like a sleazy barfly and it was a mistake to try to lure him, or whatever you're calling it. And you chose to ignore me. So, anyway, no, I'm not surprised. Next question. What was it again?"

"Um…" She hesitated, chewing on the end of her pen. "Do you think I did it wrong?"

He glanced over. She looked perfectly serious. How the hell was he supposed to answer that?

"I mean, the outfit and everything," Mabel continued. Her hazel eyes were puzzled. "I admit I don't know how you're supposed to act when you want to be alluring, so I'm not sure what conclusions I should make here. It never really came up in my life before this. I just was who I was."

And that was what he liked about her.

"Even reading the tips, I still don't really get this whole process. So, Trace, tell me the truth. Was it me? Did I telegraph to Jerry that I was up for grabs, literally?"

She was approaching this like a science project. And for some reason, it infuriated him. "Of course you did! You telegraphed sex, Mabel. *S-E-X*. What did you think would happen if you went out vamping in that outfit? You go in there like a sex Popsicle, someone's going to want to take a lick.''

''That's disgusting. Not the sex Popsicle. Actually, I kind of like that. Let me write that down.'' After a quick scribble, she raised her gaze. ''Okay, so what you're suggesting is that if I wear provocative clothes, it's all my fault if some guy paws me. Well, isn't that convenient? And I don't buy it, anyway.''

''That's not what I—''

''Because *you* saw me in that getup, and you just laughed.''

Oh, hell. How did he explain this one? *I have to laugh at you to keep my sanity?* Or at least to keep his hands off her. It made no sense to him, so he didn't know why it would to her.

''I'm different,'' he said finally.

''Uh-huh. I already knew that.'' She narrowed her eyes. ''Of course, we could just conclude that you know me too well to notice the outfit.''

Oh, he'd noticed, all right.

''Putting me aside,'' she said, ''I still don't think your theory holds water. But to test that idea, about how men just can't help themselves if women wear provocative clothes, let me pose this hypothetical.'' And then she pounced. ''When you photographed some supermodel wearing hardly anything—the one in the sand, for example—did you figure she was there for the taking?''

''No, of course not.''

''Why not?''

Mabel's convoluted logic, as well as this need to examine everything in minute detail, was making him even angrier. ''When I photograph someone, no matter what she's wearing, we both know what we're there for, and it isn't sex.''

Mabel raised an eyebrow at that one. Without saying a word, she was bringing up the kiss. Two kisses. So what? It hadn't happened with other women he'd photographed, although he didn't expect her to believe that.

''Mabel, can we drop me and my models? Why not just say you were inviting trouble when you dressed like that in a place like that? Bad combo of meat market and meat.'' He let his gaze drift over her, where she sat, so feisty, so expectant, pinned by her seat belt in his passenger seat. Her makeup was a little smeared, a lot worn away, her hair was rumpled, and she looked like anything but a femme fatale. ''And let's also say you chose the wrong target. Because I don't think you exactly send out slut-puppy vibes, if you want to know the truth. The guy had to be pretty sloshed to think you were the person you were pretending to be.''

''Oh.''

He'd thought he was being reassuring, but she didn't look happy about it.

''Well,'' she said finally, ''I guess that means I have to try again.''

''Mabel!'' He jerked the car to a stop outside her building. ''What the hell are you talking about?''

She shrugged, reaching for the door handle, angling herself out of the BMW. ''This was hardly a good test. I picked the wrong clothes, I picked the wrong place, and I picked the wrong victim—someone who was apparently predisposed to misbehave.''

''Mabel, you can't.'' Lord only knew what scheme

she'd come up with next. "Get back in here. Let's talk about this."

"Want to come up?" she asked cheerfully, dipping her head back in the door. "We can talk about it upstairs. Because if I don't get out of this ridiculous outfit within the next two minutes I swear I'm going to break out in hives. I smell like a distillery, I'm wet, I'm melting under this jacket, and I have *got* to get out of these clothes."

What was that he'd said about her not sending out slut-puppy vibes? "Mabel..."

But she was already backtracking toward the front door of her building.

"Come on!" she called back. "You might as well help decide how to fix this. You'll have to be there, too, you know. Somebody has to take the pictures."

Trace reluctantly turned off the ignition and followed her. He had no desire to sit there while Mabel "changed into something more comfortable," although he knew her well enough to believe it really would be something more comfortable. Still, she was right. If she was bound and determined to try again, he'd better participate.

Or else she would be standing nude on the Kennedy Expressway at rush hour, just to prove her point.

If he survived this "undercover odyssey," he would be very surprised.

HER HAIR WAS STILL WET from her quickie shower, but she felt tons better out of that awful leather outfit, which was lying in a heap in the bathtub. If she never saw leather again, it would be too soon.

Glancing down at her baggy cotton robe, she wondered how bad she looked. *Oh, Mabel. Like it matters.*

Still, the atmosphere was tense, to say the least. Trace was moody and sullen, and she kept thinking about the fact that it was late, that they were alone in the small apartment, that she was a lot more turned-on here, in her clumsy bathrobe, in her own home, than she had been in skimpy leather at The Hog & Heifer.

"Okay," she said, rising from the couch, refusing to think about such things. She'd tarted herself up tonight, as tarty as she could get, and all he'd done was laugh at her. That and rescue her from the clutches of an idiot when she was too feeble to do it herself.

No, Trace clearly wasn't attracted anymore, if he ever had been. Right now, he seemed to be treating her like his bratty kid sister; like someone he had to wise up and warn and keep from falling off cliffs.

Lovely. Under the circumstances, she certainly couldn't make a move on Trace—the whole idea was ludicrous—so she had better get him out of here before she got any more warm and runny than she already was.

"Then we're agreed," she said briskly. "Following Tip #37, 'Try a new place, Grace,' we've come up with somewhere I've never been, somewhere new and different, which will, incidentally, make an excellent backdrop for photos. So we will be attending the opening of the much-publicized Ulriika sculpture show at the Varsagud Gallery. And I will try for a classier look. Tomorrow night."

"No," he said grimly, "we are not agreed."

"The gallery was your idea!"

"Yes, it was," he admitted. "But only under duress. I think you already tested your 'hot' persona well enough, thank you very much. More than well enough. You almost got us both into a barroom brawl. What can you possibly do for an encore?"

"Oh, come on. If I don't have anything better than a stupid wrestling match to put in my article, I'll never get the job." She shook her head, sending little droplets every which way, showering Trace. "Sorry."

"'S okay," he mumbled, wiping a hand across his brow. But his gaze was steady, enigmatic, unsettling.

Please don't look at me like that—or I will drop my robe and climb into your lap and make a mess of both our lives.

She spun the other way. What was wrong with him, anyway? He seemed furious with her, quietly seething. But why? He'd won! She'd had to grovel, to come right out and admit that her first plan, the whole Hog & Heifer project, had been misguided and foolish. Besides, she'd let him save her from the altercation, which was a serious blow to her pride, *and* she had accepted his suggestion of a fancy art gallery for "Wild Side, Part Deux." He should be saying "I told you so" all over the place, crowing with victory.

She wasn't exactly sure why he wasn't.

Instead, he was glowering at her with enough heat to ignite her from across the room. And she just wasn't good at this. She didn't know how to interpret signals or read minds or play seduction games.

All she knew was that she wanted Trace Cameron more than anything she'd ever wanted. And she had no idea who he really was, inside. Or what he wanted from his life.

Did he see himself with a house in the suburbs, a minivan and a couple of kids? Or on a yacht off the French Riviera, with some topless bimbo on his arm?

Or maybe in a high-powered relationship with a media mogul like Rita Devon, jetting off to Milan tomorrow, and Paris the day after.

Whatever it was he wanted, she knew there was no Plain Jane, or Plain Mabel, in the picture. It just didn't fit.

"If I write my 'ho-hum-to-hot' article based on tonight," she said, breaking the strained silence, "I'll be telling *Real Men* readers they're better off staying 'ho-hum.' What kind of conclusion is that for a makeover story?"

"Maybe it's what they need to hear."

"Well, it won't thrill Sophia, I can promise you that. Which means I'll never get the job, and I'll be stuck in this place for the rest of my life, hiding my cat from the authorities, eating hot dogs, and generally being a very unhappy person. So I have to do better! I have to try again. Why won't you admit that?"

Abruptly, Trace rose from the couch, grabbed his jacket and camera bag, and headed for the door. "I'm just the Photo Boy. What do I know?"

"Don't act so gloomy. This is good news," she announced acidly. "If this works, we'll be done. You can go develop your pictures, and I can write my story, and we'll never have to see each other again."

"Good."

"Great."

"Perfect." He slammed out. "I'll pick you up at eight.

Letting out a frustrated yell, Mabel fell back onto the sofa. Why did he have to be so difficult?

But he had saved her tonight, whether she liked it or not. And maybe she had misunderstood his motives, his irritation, his moodiness. He was impossible. Especially for someone who'd spent her formative years editing the school newspaper instead of communing with the opposite sex.

Sure, she'd dated. She'd dated a whole bunch of boys—and then men—who were as socially inept as she was.

When they'd wanted a date, they'd mumbled, "D'ya wanna go out sometime?" And when they'd wanted to go further, they'd mumbled, "D'ya wanna, y'know, do it?"

Not too hard to figure out. But Trace was a whole new ball-game.

She ran to the door. "Trace?"

Too late.

THE CLOCK STRUCK EIGHT and the doorbell rang.

He was punctual, she'd give him that.

As nervous as her cat, Mabel swept to the door. If last night she was in full Biker Chick regalia, tonight she had chosen the Starlet stack of tips.

Wearing a long, clingy red slip-dress from Jane Kuku, with the addition of big hair temporarily streaked red, courtesy of Jean-Paul, and some really wicked fake nails, Mabel thought she looked drop-dead sexy, but in a classier way. As an added plus, this time she was brave enough to wear her contacts and witness her appearance in detail. She still liked the look, even in sharp focus, but she couldn't help a nervous nibble on her scarlet lipstick as she opened the door.

It was one thing to impress her mirror. But what would *he* think?

She stood there in the doorway, a little awkward, trying to strut her stuff without appearing obvious.

"You look great," Trace said softly. And for once, his eyes told the same story as his mouth.

Mabel smiled, feeling herself blossom under his gaze. She knew there was no way she compared to any of the women he knew in his professional life, but her heart told her, just this once, that his admiration was sincere.

"Thanks," she responded. "You, too. I mean, you know what you look like. But it's pretty impressive."

That went without saying. Trace just happened to be one of those guys who looked good in whatever he wore. But dressed up, with a tailored black jacket over a finely knit sweater, the Italian-silk kind, he looked *scrumptious*.

She felt the same electric charge she always felt when she was in his presence, as if all it would take was one small touch and she'd start to crackle and spark.

Might as well enjoy the fireworks while they lasted, because, she reminded herself, tonight was the last time she'd ever see him.

He was such a pain in the neck most of the time that the idea should make her happy. It didn't. Resolute, Mabel joined him in the hallway. "Time to get going," she said, with all the cheer she could muster. "The Varsagud Gallery awaits."

The gallery was in the middle of a very artsy enclave in the River North area. They had a bit of a squabble over where to park, but the BMW *was* his, so he got to decide—even if Mabel was quite sure she knew the area a heck of a lot better than he did.

As per agreement, they entered separately just in

case any lurable prospects were watching. Trace went first, toting his cameras, and Mabel watched him disappear inside with some trepidation. Elegant and at ease, he would definitely look like he belonged there. She wondered idly if there was anywhere he would look out of place. None she could think of, anyway.

And here, well, no one would think it was odd for a photographer to be snapping away at a chic gallery opening.

"My turn," she said out loud. Straightening her spine, she held her head high and sauntered in like the Queen of Sheba. Or at least the queen's third handmaiden from the left.

8

Tip #48: Dangle your key, Dee.

Remember your new attitude—you are woman!
Roar! You don't have to wait around for him to
ask you back to his place. Guys love it when
you make the first move. So if you're interested,
slide your key his way and see what happens.

AS SOON AS SHE CLEARED the door, she knew he'd
been right to choose this place. It couldn't have been
more different from The Hog & Heifer if the two had
been on different planets.

The Varsagud Gallery was very white, with high
ceilings, a lot of glass, and track lighting to show off
the artwork. A string quartet played soft music in one
corner, and waiters in tailcoats circulated with trays
of champagne.

A few paintings dotted the walls here and there,
but the big attraction was the sculpture display. Big,
weird, very avant-garde, it took center stage.

Even though she had her contacts in this time, Mabel still squinted at the large, brightly colored lump
in the center of the main room. What was it supposed
to be?

A woman wearing a dress that looked like it had

been fashioned from black paper bags handed her a program as she entered, and Mabel glanced at it. Ulriika. Sculpture. Fine Art. That was all it said.

How very pretentious. She kept that to herself, however, taking a glass of champagne when a waiter offered it, getting her bearings in these elegant, snobbish surroundings.

Around her, affluent patrons sipped fine wine, buzzing among themselves as they wandered around the sculptures. Most of the women were wearing long dresses, and a few of the men even had tuxes on. At first she was afraid they were all couples, and that her mission would be stymied again tonight. But no, there were singles, too, and they were looking around for potential companions as obviously as she was. This was definitely a better class of men than she'd seen at The Hog & Heifer.

Not quite ready to mingle, Mabel stared thoughtfully at what she'd mentally described as a "lump." The base material looked like different shades of Play-Doh, and the sculptor had attached Barbie and Ken dolls, wires, old light switches, and crushed soda cans to it. Hmm. Ugly, but entertaining. She always had liked Play-Doh.

"Are you enjoying the show?" asked a handsome, dark-haired man to her right. He had a hint of an accent, and he looked and sounded very Continental, in an old-fashioned way.

Mabel smiled at him in a way she hoped was mildly encouraging. Nothing too forward.

He raised his wine flute to his lips. "I always enjoy Ulriika's pieces. She shows such struggle, such conflict in her work, don't you think?"

"Oh, sure. Of course." She scrutinized the Play-

Doh mound more carefully, but all she saw was junk.
"Conflict. That's it on the button."

"Eduardo," he introduced himself, extending a
hand. "I paint."

"Mabel. I write."

"Ahh. It makes me want to weep."

"The fact that I'm a writer makes you want to
weep?" she asked, wondering whether she needed to
make a quick exit.

"No, of course not." He gestured toward the lump.
"This wonderful piece of art."

"Really?" The only emotional connection she got
was a reminder to recycle.

"It so clearly demonstrates man's inhumanity to
man, or in this case, to woman," he mused, his face
thoughtful as he bent closer to the clay-and-plastic
monstrosity.

Mabel was beginning to think he was putting her
on. He seemed serious, however.

"The sexual imagery is just stunning," he mar-
veled.

This time she couldn't play along. "That I don't
see at all. It looks very nonsexual to me."

He turned to her, shocked. "But the Barbie is being
dominated, submerged, by her desire for Ken. Look.
He has clothes, and she doesn't. And the wires and
switch plates show the electricity between them. Sex
and destruction in one fell swoop. It's brilliant."

Mabel tried to see what he was pointing to. She
hadn't been required to come up with plausible-
sounding symbolism since her first year of English
Lit. At the moment it seemed more stupid than plau-
sible.

Her companion smiled. "You don't agree?"

"Sometimes a Barbie is just a Barbie," she offered, and was gratified to see him laugh.

Eduardo turned out to be quite charming and very sweet. Patiently, he guided her from room to room, explaining his take on the other pieces created by the "brilliant" Ulriika.

Mabel began to relax. It was going so well. Sure, the artwork was dopey, but she enjoyed chatting with Eduardo, sipping her champagne, trying to figure out what the heck the artist was trying to say.

Even better, this was actually something she could write about, because she never would have had the guts to walk into a place like this and talk to someone like Eduardo without the smashing dress and hair and fingernails. Her *Real Men* makeover *had* given her confidence and moxie. And it had certainly caught Eduardo's eye, exactly as advertised!

Trace was out there somewhere, keeping a respectable distance, and she did her best to pretend he wasn't there. That lasted until she and Eduardo happened to pause before another piece of art—this one a card table and chairs, with mannequin heads in the chairs, and what she thought she recognized as a Hungry Hungry Hippos board game glued to the table.

As they lingered there, Trace and his camera moved nearer. Within a few clicks, he was close enough to begin to bother her.

Eduardo didn't seem to notice, droning on about Ulriika's witty critique of modern materialism and simultaneous cry for help for endangered species.

Mabel distinctly heard Trace snort his disdain, and she gave him a dark look that she hoped he understood. *Butt out.*

His eyes followed her, even more closely than his

camera. What was that he was trying to tell her? And how did he manage to insinuate himself into every waking moment of her life? A mere glance from Trace could turn her on from across the room, while standing very close to handsome, articulate Eduardo did absolutely nothing.

"Go away," she mouthed back.

He gave her a lazy smile, and pointed to the table.

"What?" she asked silently.

Trace rustled around in his bag, removing a small square of paper. And then he began to search for a pen.

Wheeling away, Mabel pasted on a smile. "I'm sorry, Eduardo. Did you say something?"

"That photographer seems very insistent," Eduardo noted absently. "Do you know him?"

"Uh, not exactly." Mabel managed a short laugh. "I'm not sure."

"It's of no importance. Shall we...?" her companion asked, indicating they should move on to the next piece in the exhibit.

But as they skirted around the Hungry Hungry Hippos, Trace managed to just catch her hand, passing her a small, scrunched-up note before she could stop him. *Heavens.* She was trying to be so sophisticated, and he was acting like they were in a high-school study hall.

At least Eduardo appeared not to have noticed.

As he offered his theory on what a tower of damaged Rubik's Cubes was supposed to mean, Mabel very carefully unfolded the note.

Make love on the table, Mabel?

Her mind filled with images before she could stop it. She saw herself scattering hippos to the four winds as Trace wrapped her in his embrace, pressing her down onto that flimsy card table.

"Make love on the table, Mabel...."

Damn him to hell. She actually wanted to.

Quickly, she crumpled the note in her fist, dropping it harmlessly to the floor, kicking it under the Rubik's Cubes. Now it was part of the artwork, and people could search for symbolism in that.

And if Trace was lurking out there somewhere, she planned to try very hard not to notice.

After that, she made an effort to be attentive and charming to Eduardo, laughing at his jokes, smiling up at him, letting him lean closer than was absolutely necessary.

"What do you think of this one?" he inquired politely, leading her into a small side room containing only one piece.

Mabel took a gander and her eyes widened. She was staring at a huge reclining nude. Most of it was three-dimensional and appeared to be plaster, with luscious, curving hips and legs, and an oversize head, tricked out to suggest Marilyn Monroe. But just below the shoulders, a flat, wooden, luridly painted cutout of her bust was attached, with a flashing fifty-watt bulb set in the center of each breast.

"Oh. Dear. Well, I..."

She broke off in midsputter. As if the mammoth mammo-sculpture wasn't bad enough, Trace's head was hovering just above Marilyn's glow-in-the-dark bosom.

What was he doing? Besides sending her a look dark enough to burn out both of Marilyn's lightbulbs.

There was no way she could ignore him *there*. He mouthed something she couldn't catch, pointing at her and then back at himself. Whatever his problem was, he looked serious, and she could tell from his hand signals that he wanted her to hightail it around there to share a conference behind Marilyn Monroe's creamy plaster buttocks.

Furtively she shook her head, trying to indicate that she was doing fine with Eduardo and didn't want to be disturbed, without tipping Eduardo off that she was having a conversation with the busybody photographer across the room.

But Trace wouldn't give up. His lips formed the word *now* very clearly and he pointed again. *You. Me. Now.*

Oh, brother. If this was an excuse to hand off another "Make love on the table, Mabel," she swore she'd smack him, right there behind Marilyn.

"Will you excuse me for a moment?" she asked Eduardo. "I have to, uh…" She made a quick, ambiguous gesture, hoping he would assume she had to go to the rest room.

"But of course," he said, bowing slightly from the waist.

Mabel was impressed. She'd never met a man who bowed before. It was like something from a movie.

But she still had to get him out of the way. She gave him an apologetic smile. "I'll meet you up front, near the musicians, in five minutes. How does that sound?"

"Perfect." He took her hand gently in his, and pressed his lips to the back of it.

Wasn't that sweet? There was no chemistry there

whatsoever, but heck, she had to give extra points to a guy who bowed and kissed her hand.

With a small wave, she pretended to head back toward the main room with the Play-Doh sculpture, ducking behind a pillar long enough to watch Eduardo leave the small "Marilyn" room. Then she doubled back to find Trace.

There he was, pacing behind the supine nude, looking angry and impatient and altogether fit to be tied.

"What do you think you're doing?" they both demanded in unison.

Mabel struck first. "What was that stupid note for? 'Make love on the table, Mabel'? And why were you trying to flag me down? I felt like a 747 on the tarmac at O'Hare!"

"I was trying to tell you that I have plenty of pictures," he retorted. She noted he had conveniently avoided any excuse for his bean-headed rhyme. "I have a whole roll of great shots of you and Count Dracula clinking glasses over the Barbie burial mound. And I have another roll of your heads together over the Rubik's Cubes, looking oh-so-cozy. With those in the bank, there's no need for you to be hanging all over that guy anymore."

"I wasn't hanging all over anybody. I was trying to have a conversation, which I can hardly do with you waving your arms like a semaphore! You were supposed to leave me alone to do my job, remember?"

"Aw, come on," he said fiercely. "Conversation? You were giving out come-hither signals like nobody's business."

"I was not. We were looking at art. We were talking about art." The fact that the art in question had lightbulbs on its breasts did not escape her, although she wished it would. "As for come-hithering, well, even if I were, which I wasn't, isn't that what I was supposed to be doing? How do you lure a lover without come-hithering?"

"Mabel, you know as well as I do you don't have to take it that far." He clenched his jaw so tightly she could see a muscle twitch in his cheek. "You're supposed to look attractive, and I take pictures, and then we're done. Vamoose, scram. I don't think anyone intended for you to go picking up guys for real."

"I don't think that's any of your business," she said stiffly. "If you've taken enough pictures for tonight, then *you* are free to vamoose and/or scram, whenever you please."

"I'm not scramming until you dump Romeo over there and get out of this place."

"I'm an adult, and so is 'Romeo.' I like him. I like *me,* this way," she lied shamelessly. "Eduardo and I are enjoying each other's company, and I don't see any reason for the evening to end. I'm going to take another one of the fifty tips, and 'dangle my key, Dee.'"

"Mabel," Trace said, and she could tell he was quietly, coldly furious. "You can do whatever damn foolish thing you want. But I don't have to watch it. And if I leave, I hope you realize that there won't be anyone there to punch out your Romeos, or to haul your butt out of the line of fire."

"I'm a big girl. I don't need you or anyone else to rescue me." She crossed her arms over the clingy red dress, the dress that looked better than anything she'd ever worn. Fat lot of good that did her. "I never did need you."

"Fine."

"Great!" she shouted after him.

"Perfect," he muttered, but he didn't look back.

"Yeah, that's right. You took your pictures. Time to hit the road, Jack. Isn't that what you usually do?"

But Trace was striding away from her so fast she wasn't sure he even heard.

And Marilyn Monroe's flat wooden breasts just kept blinking.

Mabel stood there for a second, in front of the hideous sculpture, composing herself. Why did it seem like every time she turned around, there was an animal-print thong, a dominatrix corset, an oversize nude movie star with a hundred-watt bosom, to remind her how hopelessly unhip, unhot, she was?

"Well, no more, sweetheart!" she said out loud, saluting Marilyn in all her naked glory.

Mabel spun on her spike heel, heading for the main room of the gallery, where she had every intention of meeting Eduardo.

And every intention of dangling her key. If *Real Men* wanted her to live dangerously and "walk on the wild side," then, damn it, she would do just that.

The string quartet was playing a song from an old Fred Astaire movie—the one where Ginger was washing her hair and Fred sang about how much he loved her, just the way she looked tonight. It made her sad to think of it, and she tuned it out.

"Eduardo!" she called out, moving to his side before she lost her nerve, hastening to accept the glass of champagne he offered.

She had to hold herself firmly in control not to check over her shoulder. Was Trace there somewhere, watching her every move, poised to jump in and throttle this one, too, if she chickened out?

"I hope so," she said under her breath. She wanted him to see her when she *didn't* chicken out.

"Hope what, my dear?" Eduardo inquired.

"I'm hoping that you'll come back to my apartment for a moment," she declared suddenly. "Would you like to join me in a nightcap?"

Eduardo paused, looking quite surprised. But after a moment, he said, "Yes, yes, of course." He emptied his flute with one swallow and offered his arm. "Shall we?"

She linked her arm through his, putting on a brave face as they swept out the front doors of the Varsagud Gallery. It was only as they reached his Range Rover that she wondered what the heck she thought she was doing.

She didn't even know this man. He could be a jerk, a criminal, a serial killer.

Eduardo politely helped her with her seat belt, pulling away from the parking lot at about ten miles an hour. Okay, so probably not a serial killer. She ventured a nervous glance his way. Why had she been so foolish? Pride was a terrible, debilitating thing. Just to get back at Trace, she'd leaped off the side of a cliff. Now she didn't have a rope to rappel back up there.

"You're very quiet," he noted.

"Just enjoying the evening." She made an effort to be perkier, offering a foolproof conversation starter. "So, tell me about your work."

That was all she needed to get him started on an energetic lecture about every dab of paint he'd ever laid on a canvas. Mabel interceded to say "Turn right" or "Next left" every once in a while, but otherwise he seemed happy to fill the silence all by himself.

But then Eduardo halted, peering out the windshield of his car. "Have I taken a wrong turn? Is this really where you live?"

"Yes, this is it. My apartment building is right there," she assured him, pointing the way.

Eduardo faced her with a dismayed expression. "But where will I park my car? Is this safe?"

She didn't think the neighborhood looked *that* bad. You couldn't see any of the gang graffiti from here, and a couple of the streetlights were burned out, disguising other evidence of urban blight. "I live here, after all. *I* think it's safe."

"All right," he said reluctantly, pulling the car over. As soon as he let her out, he locked it up like a safe and set a steering-wheel bar and a door alarm.

"It really is safe," she said again.

"Of course it is." But he kept sending nervous glances over his shoulder, as if he expected to be mugged any second, and he glued himself to Mabel's side.

She didn't know whether he really thought she could protect him or it was some kind of ploy to get close, but she hustled to get him upstairs before he saw any more of the area and really freaked out.

"Let me get that for you," he murmured, covering her hand with his, taking the key.

Mabel took a step back. Was it just her, or was it icky for a man to push you out of the way and manhandle your key?

"Uh, thanks," she said dubiously, following him

into her own home, switching on every light available just so he didn't get the wrong idea.

The wrong idea? She'd invited him back to her place for a nightcap. What other idea was there?

"It is delightful," Eduardo announced, glancing around. "I see what you've done here. I love the irony, the cynicism."

She thought it was just a low-rent apartment, and he was looking for artistic statements.

"Aha! The whole decor sends such messages about suburban bourgeois attitudes.... Hmm. So very kitschy, isn't it?"

"'Kitschy'?" She wasn't sure, but she thought that meant tacky.

"Yes, yes. It is so purposefully tacky, so Bohemian, perhaps jejune. How very—" he strained "—refreshing. Reminiscent of a Parisian artist's garret, yes?"

She had to give him credit for coming up with something remotely positive when he looked about as uncomfortable as if someone had just dumped a fish down his pants. "Purposefully tacky" but "refreshing"? Why did she suddenly have this image of her apartment as a pack of chewing gum?

"Why don't you sit down?" she asked, vaguely waving him toward the sofa. "Would you like something to drink? I have..." She considered what was available. "Lemonade, water, or diet pop." Not exactly fine wine or cocktails. Nary a Perrier nor a cognac to be found.

"Water, thank you," he responded, giving her a thin smile.

Poor Eduardo, trying to make the best of things. She set his glass of water on the table in front of him, wondering whether he'd noticed the cartoon-cat coaster and whether that, too, was kitsch. Undoubtedly. Mable perched next to him on the sofa, carefully sipping her own lemonade, but she wasn't really paying attention.

"Mmm-hmm," she said, agreeing with whatever he said that she hadn't heard, but she itched to get to the bedroom and find her notebook. Since that would clearly be rude, she tried out phrases in her mind, toying with how she could best word her newest observation.

Subject from experiment number two hates my apartment and thinks I'm a philistine, but is apparently attracted enough to overlook what he perceives as my shortcomings. Conclusion: This must count as a successful lure.

Meanwhile, ole MIQ thought dress was nice, but otherwise showed no signs of anything but a fit of pique.

Where did that come from? Trace—or MIQ, as he had become in her journal—was not an official responder to her relative lurability or lack thereof, and never had been. He needed to get out of her thoughts and out of her notebook. Now.

Mabel sat up straight as Eduardo's hand plunked onto her knee. He looked very intent, expectant, and he edged closer on the couch.

She backed up, slipping out from under his hand, wondering what the heck he'd just said. "I—I'm sorry. Could you repeat that?"

"I asked," Eduardo whispered, advancing again,

this time sliding his other hand onto her other knee, "who *is* Mabel?"

The way he said her name, it sounded like "Maybelle," like some twangy singer at the Grand Ole Opry.

"Yes, Mabel," he continued, inching along until his hip bumped her, until her back hit the arm of the couch. He took the lemonade from her hand and set it on the coffee table along with his water. "I find you a fascinating bundle of contradictions."

Although she was distracted by that glass of lemonade plopped onto her coffee table without a coaster under it, she responded, "I don't think I'm all that fascinating, but thank you just the same."

"So elegant, but so unsophisticated." His voice dropped even lower, but his fingers crept higher. "So eager and so hesitant. It's very beguiling, Mabel."

"W-well, thank you. I think." She was having a hard time thinking with his hand there, as she tried to decide what the modern siren did under these circumstances. Was it unpardonably rude to slap a man? How about shoving him off the couch?

"Mabel," he murmured, dipping his head and coming in for the kill.

"I have to, uh…" she said brightly, leaping to her feet, accidentally clonking him in the head with her elbow. "Oh, I'm so sorry! Let me…"

She was sorry she'd hurt him, but not sorry to escape. Quickly, she ran off to the kitchen for a cool cloth and an aspirin.

Oddly enough, Eduardo followed. Apparently disregarding his head injury, he was smiling. "You amuse me, Mabel, when you play the coquette."

Was that what she was doing? She smiled weakly,

trying to fend him off, but she was trapped up against the counter in the tiny kitchen. "I don't think this is a good idea," she tried.

With one hand over the red lump on his brow, Eduardo moved closer. And then stopped dead. "Oh, my God." His eyes went wide with horror, focusing on a spot over her shoulder. "Oh, my God," he said again, louder this time. He looked as if he were having a heart attack right there.

"What is it?" Mabel scanned the area behind her. There was nothing there but her refrigerator. The fridge? What was so amazing about that?

"Those magnets," he rasped. "They are..."

"Fun?" she supplied. "Different?"

He shook his head.

"Okay, well, how about kitschy? Tacky? Refreshing?"

But Eduardo kept shaking his head, stumbling backward. "They...they strike fear into my heart," he whispered.

Since a big heap of Play-Doh had almost made him cry, she didn't suppose it was too weird that a few magnets scared him witless. But still...

"I collect refrigerator magnets," she explained, backing up and pointing to a few favorites. "These are The Brady Bunch. See? Marcia, Greg, Jan...even Alice. It's pretty rare to find a whole, complete set like that at a garage sale, but I did."

"G-garage sale?" he echoed.

"Uh-huh. I suppose that's where Ulriika got the spare Barbie parts and plastic hippos, don't you?"

"Ulriika? At a garage sale? I don't think so," he hissed, drawing himself up.

Snob. Mabel couldn't help remembering that Trace

had appreciated her magnets. *"I always liked Jan better than Marcia, didn't you?"*

Funny, the things that drew people together. She hadn't said a thing about it at the time, but yes, she did prefer Jan. Always had. How strange to have something in common with him, when their worlds were so very different.

She shook it off. *No more thoughts about MIQ.*

She busied herself giving a tour of her prized magnets. "These over here," she continued, indicating a foiled assortment, "look just like the real chocolate kisses and miniature candy bars. I got those at a swap meet."

Eduardo shuddered.

Enjoying herself, Mabel kept up the show. "This pink one is an ice-cream sundae, complete with spoon, and over on this side, I've got a different magnet for every year the Bulls won a championship. Oh, and these—they're reminders of places I've visited. The tulip is from Holland, Michigan, the tractor is from Peoria, and the Abe Lincoln head is, of course, from New Salem."

"A veritable travelogue," he replied in a shaky voice. "Perhaps we could return to the other room now?"

"Sure. You go right ahead. I'll bring your aspirin and be there in a sec."

As he retreated in a rush, Mabel smiled. Her taste in decor seemed to be just what the doctor ordered to dampen Eduardo's ardor. By the time she got out to the living room with his aspirin, she felt sure he would have thought up a convenient excuse to leave.

Her own head was pounding, and she hadn't taken an elbow to the temple. Hastily, Mabel swallowed a couple of aspirin herself before setting one on a small plate for Eduardo. She might have been ignorant of the ways of men when she started this assignment, but she was learning fast. Yes, she told herself, Eduardo would be scrambling to find a way out now.

Sailing out of the kitchen alcove, she almost crashed into him.

"*Cara mia,*" he murmured, hauling her up against the wall and knocking the plate from her hand. In a flash, his lips were attached like a suction cup on her neck, and his hands were roaming absolutely everywhere.

Ooops. Didn't see that coming.

9

Tip #29: Moan on the phone, Joan.

Erotic phone fun is easy and practically fool-proof, even for shy girls. Remember—you're all alone, in the comfort of your own room, and you can say whatever outrageous, sexy things pop into your fertile little brain. And if you're stumped as to what sweet nothings to whisper to your long-distance lover, follow our guidelines below. He may not see you, but he'll feel you all over....

"EDUARDO, PLEASE, DON'T. I don't think this is a good idea," she managed, wriggling away.

She'd barely begun to disconnect herself when she heard a loud, high-pitched, decidedly feline "rrr-owwww" that split the stuffy air. As Eduardo screamed and clutched his ankle, there was a flash of fur, and another, lower growl.

Polly was nowhere to be seen, but Eduardo seemed to dive backward, smashing into the opposite wall, hopping on one foot, landing in a heap.

She couldn't help it. It really was funny. Her commando cat had swooped in and saved the day, perhaps just to let Mabel know the bowl was empty, or maybe even to protect Mabel's honor.

As she covered her mouth with one hand, giggling through her fingers, Eduardo rose stiffly, limping badly.

"I'm so sorry," she offered, trying to help him, but he looked less than amused.

"Circumstances conspire against us," he told her grimly, nursing the lump on his head with one hand and his injured leg with the other.

"Yes, I think they do." She didn't know what else to say except *thank goodness,* and that didn't seem very nice.

"I think perhaps we should call it a night." He winced as he tried to walk down the hall under his own steam.

"Oh, dear. I really am sorry, Eduardo, but maybe it's for the best," she admitted, trailing behind, keeping an eye out for Supercat. "You seem like a very nice person, and I enjoyed your company."

"Then why is it for the best?"

That was harder to explain. "Mostly because this whole thing—the dress, the hair, attending a chichi gallery opening—it's not me. I have a feeling it's what you're attracted to, and it's all a big fake." Actually, once she got started, it wasn't hard at all. "I don't think you'd be very interested in the real Mabel. I'm not sophisticated, I'm not an artist, I don't see anything profound about piles of Play-Doh with Barbie and Ken on top, and I'm not Bohemian or refreshing."

"Ah, but you are. Refreshing, at the very least." He smiled ruefully around his wounds. "I gather I am not what you are looking for, either."

"Oh, no, that's not—" Mabel broke off. She'd started telling the truth. Might as well keep it up. "You're right, Eduardo."

With a hand still clasped to the bump on his forehead, he arched an eyebrow. "I seem to recall a certain tension in the air when your eyes met those of the photographer at the gallery. Was I wrong? Is that the man you'd rather have gone home with tonight?"

Mabel felt her cheeks flush with a sudden heat. How embarrassing to play games with people's affections and then get found out.

"I do know him," she confessed. "You were right on that score. But there's nothing between us—nothing except what you called 'tension.' He drives me crazy. He's always knocking me off-balance—he thrives on it—and he makes me so angry."

"Ah. I see. So you are in love with him." She tried to protest, but Eduardo shook his head. "I know when I'm beaten."

Mabel took his arm as he hopped the few steps down the hall from the kitchen. "I have to say, you're a very good sport. Can I offer you a bandage, some gauze?"

"No, I don't think so." He grimaced with pain as he crossed to the door. "I think I would prefer to seek medical aid at home, where I am less likely to reinjure myself."

"I don't mind giving you a Band-Aid," she called after him.

But once he was safely out the door, Mabel let out a sigh of relief. What a mistake. She was not and never would be the sort of woman who brought home strangers. She should be counting her lucky stars she got out of it so well. *Never again.*

Slowly, she retreated to her room to get out of those shoes and that dress. The scarlet fabric pooled on the floor, and she gazed at it regretfully. The evening had turned out to be a waste of a great dress. It wasn't that she could never wear it again, just that she'd never have an occasion. She knew her social calendar. Slinky red slip dresses that hugged every inch of skin didn't fit.

"Oh, well. At least it will make a good article."

Because now she had a beginning—Plain Jane, including the problems with mascara, panty hose and coordination the day she took the assignment. A middle—attempted makeover into hot stuff, with all the outrageous anecdotes about dressing rooms and fingernails and backward teddies. And an end— Part One: Humor and Humiliation at The Hog & Heifer, and Part Two: Voilá! A Successful Transformation, with a handsome man hooked and reeled in.

It was fresh, funny, irreverent, as well as intimate, since she'd be admitting all her mistakes and how she'd worked around them. *My Makeover, or, How I Learned to Stop Worrying and Love Lingerie.* Just the sort of thing *Real Men* readers would eat up with a spoon.

But the thing that was really going to make it come alive was her conclusion. Aside from *Be careful who you put the moves on,* which fit both "wild side" experiments, she had come to a newer, more important realization.

As she formed it in her mind, it came out something like: *You can make me over all you want, but I am still the same Mabel inside.*

She might be normal looking, no glamour girl, but she liked herself that way. Sure, she could use some of the tips for fun, to enhance herself, perhaps even gain confidence in her appearance and powers of seduction. But it would never cover up, disguise, or recast the essential Mabel.

How very empowering. "Sophia is going to love this," she said to her reflection, stripped down to red panties and bra, the garter belt with the rosebuds, and the scarlet stockings.

She sat down on the bed, her head in her hands. Her story was in terrific shape—in her mind at least—and she felt certain, for the first time, that the *Real Men* job could be hers.

So why was she so miserable?

Eduardo's words came back to haunt her. *"Ah. I see. So you are in love with him."*

"Is it so terrible?" she asked herself out loud. "Can I help it if I wish it was *him* I'd dangled my key in front of tonight?"

Maybe not terrible, but definitely ridiculous. She couldn't seriously wish she'd sidled up to Trace in her sensational red dress, flirted, giggled, and asked him to come home with her. Could she?

Okay, so he had expressed a certain fondness for her cat and her magnets and her apartment—unlike Eduardo. Even though he seemed a little large for her surroundings, he sort of fit in. He'd pushed a little too close, lounged on her floor, drunk her lemonade, and made a mess on her coffee table.

But it had seemed so right somehow.

Mabel shook her head. It couldn't be.

Nothing had changed to make him someone different, to make him someone who had *not* dated the coolest, most beautiful women on the planet. Even "hotted up," Mabel knew very well she wasn't in his league.

"But what if I don't need to be in his league?" she mused.

Her mind spinning, she lay back on the bed. He did seem to be attracted, for whatever reason. The memory of that kiss was never far away. And those smoky glances, the terrible rhymes, even the "before" photo session, when he'd laid her out on the floor—it all seemed to suggest that he *did* want her.

She supposed that to him she might be some kind of one-night curiosity. Heck, maybe a one-hour curiosity. Maybe after a steady diet of supermodels and power mavens, he had a burning desire to see how normal women made love again.

"Make love on the table, Mabel?" For one hot, crazy night with Trace, she might actually consider it.

What would he have done if she'd unfolded that slip of paper and shouted "Yes!" across the room? She might be enjoying the pleasure of his company right now.

A new, even more terrifying thought struck her.

"What if it isn't just a game?"

She sat up, shocked. She'd always tried to second-guess whatever it was he said or did, assign motives, get to the root of his every ambiguity. But what if, at some level, he was as off-balance about all this as she was? What if his moodiness, his dark looks and remarks, were his way of showing that he cared, but he wasn't sure *she* did?

"Whoa, girl," she commanded herself. "Let's not get too far off the planet just yet."

But it was already too late to rein her heart in.

She'd backed off when he'd kissed her, afraid of falling for him and breaking her heart. Well, bulletin to Mabel: She had long since fallen.

So what if *she* made the move this time? What if she decided to see where a roller coaster with Trace might lead her, instead of just counting it out before she even got on the ride?

Mabel let the idea sit there in her mind for just a second, wondering whether this was possible, whether it was wise, whether she cared. And then it hit her.

"Good Lord. I'm thinking about luring a lover!"

But how?

"Where is the list?" she demanded, scrambling to a sitting position, pulling her big leather purse out from under the bed. "You would've thought I'd have the damn things memorized by now."

She shuffled through the pages, rapidly scanning the lines for something that might help. "Forget the clothes and hair tips—I've already tried most of those. I guess I could use 'Pull him into the bath, Kath' or 'Make love on a train, Jane.' Naw. I'd have to get him to the bathtub or the train first. 'Try out the gym, Kim'? Takes too long. What else is there? 'Moan on the phone, Joan.' You know, that might just do it."

It would certainly communicate what she wanted to, it was nothing like the things she'd already done, so Trace wouldn't be immunized, and the *Real Men* editors said it was foolproof.

Mabel sat on the edge of the bed, absently fanning herself with the paper. Did she have the guts for this? Well, like the tip suggested, it had to be easier to do it over the phone than face-to-face.

This was insane. And she was going to do it. Flushed, her heart beating like a tom-tom, she looked up the number for the Ritz, punching it into her cordless phone with a trembling finger.

Then she had to wait, impatient and jumpy, as the hotel operator answered and switched the call to his room.

"If he's in," she thought aloud, "that's a good sign. If he's not there, it's a bad omen, and I'll know I shouldn't have tried. And if a woman answers—" she clenched her jaw "—I'll call them back and wake them up every three minutes all night long."

Ring. Ring.

The phone was picked up on the other end.

"H'lo?" he mumbled, sounding sleepy.

Her heart leaped in her chest, and she scooted back on the bed, the phone pressed to her cheek.

"Trace, it's…meee," she breathed, stretching out the word just the way the tip had told her to.

"Mabel? You sound weird. Are you okay?"

Well, yes and no. Doing her best throaty murmur, she tried, "I'm…fiiiine."

"Then why are you calling? What is it? That guy you left with? Did something go wrong?"

She imagined him sitting up in bed to catch the phone, the white sheet pooling around his waist. She closed her eyes, but the vision wouldn't disappear.

"Mabel, tell me what's wrong. Is it the guy from the gallery?"

With her mind playing movies of Trace half naked in a sheet, the last thing she wanted to think about was Eduardo.

In a rush, she explained, "Eduardo is long gone. Nothing went wrong. Well, he hated my place, I accidentally gave him a concussion, and my cat slashed his ankle, so he was limping all the way out the door. Other than that—''

Trace laughed on the other end of the phone—a happy, carefree sound that lifted Mabel's spirits. She almost forgot she was supposed to sound breathless and enticing.

She went back to plan A. ''I—I'd rather talk about...about yoooouuuu. How are you, Traaaace?''

The instructions said to use his name a lot, so she was trying. Plus, make it gaspy, raspy, barely audible, slow and drawn out, emphasize words with *s,* and include sexy-sounding words like *tantalize* and *delicious.* This wasn't easy.

''I can hardly hear you,'' he said loudly. ''Speak up, will you?''

''I can't!'' she snapped, before she recovered her husky tone.

''Mabel, what is this all about? It's been a long day, and a long night, and I'm tired.''

''Were you...assssleep? It's sssso...late. I hope I didn't...waaake you, Traaace. I was thinking of...yoooouu. *Delicious, tantalizing* thoughts.''

She rolled her eyes. This was so stupid. And if he didn't get it now, he never would.

''Mabel, I can't hear you. You sound awful—like you're having trouble breathing. Are you sure you're not sick? Do you have a sore throat?''

Sick? Oh, brother. ''Yessss, I'm ssssure. I'm sssso fine.''

''I think you must be coming down with something. Get off the phone and take your temperature, okay? A fever would explain why you're not making sense, and laryngitis or strep would cover what's wrong with your voice. So take your temp, and if it's over one hundred, call me back. Otherwise, you should try to get some sleep.'' He actually sounded concerned. ''If I don't hear from you, I'll check with you in the morning to see if you're feeling any better. G'night, Mabel. Sweet dreams.''

And he hung up.

He hung up!

Totally humiliated, Mabel fell headlong back into her bed and pulled her pillow over her head. She was trying to be sexy, and he thought she had strep throat! Maybe if she was lucky, she'd suffocate before he called back.

TRACE SAT THERE IN HIS bed at the Ritz, the fine Irish bed-linens pooled in his lap. He should just go back to sleep, like he'd said he was going to. But somehow he didn't think he'd be able to doze off.

Fully awake now, he gazed thoughtfully at the phone, wondering what the hell he had just listened to.

That had been so bizarre it wasn't funny. Well, it was funny. But he didn't think Mabel had intended to be funny.

So what had she intended?

He ran a hand through his hair and stared at the ceiling. She'd sure sounded weird, but she'd said she wasn't sick. Not sick, yet she had slurred speech, inability to concentrate, labored breathing.... If it were anyone else, he'd come up with the obvious conclusion.

Drugs. Could Mabel be such a mess after her date with that creepy Romeo that she'd resort to sleeping pills?

Suddenly alarmed, Trace reached for his pants. But

he stopped with one leg in. *No way Mabel is popping pills because she had a disastrous date.*

He would stake his life on that one. So what was this all about?

As he pulled on his pants the rest of the way, Trace replayed the conversation, searching for a clue. She'd sounded odd, then pretty normal when she'd synopsized what had happened with Eduardo.

His lips quirked. Trust Mabel to have a date that was more like a Keystone Kops routine. *"I accidentally gave him a concussion, my cat slashed his ankle, he limped all the way out the door...."*

Way to go, Mabel. Just what the guy deserved.

Trace felt a tiny stab of guilt at that. After all, it wasn't Romeo's fault. It was just that Trace had experienced very unwelcome feelings when he'd seen that dark, handsome man lean close to Mabel and whisper into her ear. If he didn't know himself better, he might have thought he was...jealous. Ouch.

"Not in this lifetime," he muttered.

He wasn't jealous—just concerned. Yeah, that was it. He liked Mabel. *Liked,* as in friends. And it was acceptable to be concerned when a friend sounded as if she was in trouble.

And that she had. Okay, so after the story about Eduardo's awkward exit, she'd said something like, *"But that's not why I called. I wanted to talk to you."*

Was that it? It had been so hard to hear her.

He frowned into space, concentrating hard. What came next? He felt sure she'd asked if he was asleep, and then had whispered something about it being very late. That was when she'd started to slur her words and hiss on all the *s*'s.

Suddenly, it all came back to him. Her voice

echoed in his ear, sounding oddly like Sharon Stone in *Basic Instinct.* *"I hope I didn't wake you, Trace. I was thinking of you. Delicious, tantalizing thoughts."*

Trace narrowed his eyes. But Mabel's voice hadn't reminded him of Sharon Stone at the time. Mabel had sounded more like she'd drunk too much cold medicine.

"I hope I didn't wake you, Trace. I was thinking of you. Delicious, tantalizing thoughts."

Her words hung there, seductive and portentous, winding themselves around his brain until he couldn't ignore the obvious anymore.

"Delicious, tantalizing…"

"Aw, jeez. How stupid can I be?" He grabbed his shirt and tossed it on over his head. "'Moan on the phone, Joan.' Tip #29. Mabel is trying the damn things out on *me.* She's trying to seduce me."

That had to be it. Feeling like an idiot, he found shoes and keys and ran out the door, determined to get to Mabel and settle this once and for all.

Was she playing him for a fool? Or did she really want to lure him into bed, using the tips the way they were intended?

Mabel didn't know a whole lot about seduction, that much was clear. Which was exactly why she would think it made sense to call him after midnight and hiss like a snake on Nyquil. Of all the women in the world, only Mabel would interpret talking dirty on the phone in that unique way. And, damn it, that was exactly why it turned him on.

Trace whipped the rented BMW around corners, squealing his tires, speeding through yellow lights. He took out a traffic cone and narrowly missed a blinking orange barricade. Too bad. He was not a patient man at the best of times. And these were not the best of times.

Screeching to a stop, he practically left the car doors open in his haste to get up to Mabel's apartment and get an answer out of her.

"Mabel!" he shouted, pounding on her door. "Mabel?"

No answer. Damn it.

"Mabel, I know you're probably upset with me, and I don't blame you. You're right—I was an idiot, and I didn't get it at first. I'm sorry. But it only took about two seconds." He paced back and forth in her hallway, carrying on a conversation with her door. "As soon as we hung up, it hit me. 'Moan on the phone, Joan.' I get it! So let me in, will you?"

No answer. Damn it.

Was she trying to make him grovel? Or was she hiding out again?

"You have to admit, you haven't exactly sent clear signals. I mean, you told me it was stupid and crazy and we were all wrong for each other and the attraction was based on lingerie, remember?"

Tactical error. He did not need to be thinking of Mabel in the little red slip right now. He was plenty hot without that extra bit of incentive.

"And then I practically had to handcuff myself to keep my hands off the black leather outfit. But I did it. Because that was the way you wanted it. And tonight—you left the gallery with that Eduardo hand-kissing moron. How was I supposed to know you'd changed your mind?"

But Mabel wasn't responding. Trace laid a hand against the worn wood of her door. "Mabel," he said more softly, more persuasively, "open the door. We can talk about this."

Although if he had his way, they wouldn't be doing a whole lot of talking once he got in there.

His voice rose, and he hit his fist on the door. "Mabel, if you're stalling again, like you were in that damn dressing room, I'm going to throttle you."

No answer. *Damn it.*

"All right. That's it. Either open the door right now, or I'm going to kick it in."

He stood back, far enough to clear the door. He gave her ten seconds, counting slowly, but she still didn't show.

"Aw, jeez." He didn't want to have to do this. When his tempestuous relationship with Rita had ended, after too many vases had been thrown, too many pictures ripped to bits, too many plates and goblets shattered, he had vowed never to let himself descend to that level of passion again.

No more entanglements with women he worked with. No more out-of-control, dangerous desires.

So much for his vows.

Now, here he was, standing all by himself in a low-rent-apartment hallway, contemplating smashing down a door to get to a woman.

Inside, Mabel might be waiting in the red teddy, or the black garter belt with the fishnet stockings. *"I hope I didn't wake you, Trace. I was thinking of you. Delicious, tantalizing thoughts."*

"The hell with it."

And he kicked it in. It splintered off the hinges with the first blow.

"Mabel?"

No sign of her. The living room was dark and quiet,

although Polly did come meowing along, bumping her head into his hand.

Carefully, Trace turned on a light, but it didn't help much. Then he set the door back into the doorframe, propping it up with a kitchen stool, so at least the cat couldn't get out. He hoped stray burglars would also be discouraged, although they'd have to be pretty lousy burglars.

It didn't matter. In the mood he was in, he could have strangled any ten robbers with his bare hands and not even worked up a sweat.

Glancing around the empty living room, he knew now that he had wasted his words. He'd recited his monologue without benefit of an audience.

Yes, he was definitely a fool. A fool for love.

In the still apartment, he could hear the pipes creak, and a rush of water coming from the back of the apartment. The shower.

Without thinking, Trace strode down the hall, yanked open the door, and burst in.

He could see the silhouette of her slim, curvy body through the shower curtain. *"Delicious, tantalizing thoughts..."*

Mabel turned. She let out a squeal, snatching back the curtain, protecting herself with its folds, as water sprayed out into the small bathroom. "Trace?" Her eyes sparkled with tiny droplets from her shower, but with something more, too. Desire.

She was wet, she was naked, and she was the most beautiful thing he'd ever seen. How could anyone have thought Mabel was sedate or ho-hum? She made his blood race in his veins, his temperature rise, his whole body jump to attention.

"Trace?" she whispered again.

"It's definitely me," he said, with a voice that came out so rough and ragged he would never have recognized it as his own. "I got the message, Mabel."

And then he stepped right into the tub, clothes and all. He lifted Mabel up into his embrace, he found her mouth with his own, and he wrapped his arms hard and fast around her wet, sleek, delectable curves.

10

Tip #50: Kiss and don't tell, Nell.

Secrets are sexy. Whereas tell-all tomes, ap-
pearances on talk shows to rehash your love life,
gossiping with girlfriends about his, ahem,
shortcomings are a real turnoff. Don't even
think about going there. Just smile like Mona
Lisa, and keep your seductive secrets to yourself.

MABEL WAS WET, SHE WAS naked, and she was so
overheated she fully expected steam to start rising
from the tub.

One moment she was standing alone under a cool
shower, trying desperately not to think of him, and
the next he had barged in with her, big as life, fully
clothed, as gorgeous as ever. He'd pushed into her
shower the same way he'd bulldozed himself into her
life. And there was no way in hell she was kicking
him out now.

"What are you doing here?" she whispered, in between kissing him back and holding on for dear life.
"This is fantastic! I can't believe you're real. I
thought I'd never see you again. You thought I had
strep throat. And how did you get in?"

"Mabel, no questions. Not right now." Bracketing her face with his hands, he delved into her mouth, kissing her so thoroughly she couldn't breathe, let alone think.

His lips and his tongue tasted warm, luscious, irresistible, and she couldn't stop herself from diving in, from luxuriating in the heady feel of his mouth on hers.

She'd almost forgotten she was naked until her breasts grazed his chest. Shocked, she broke away from his kiss and glanced down at her taut, eager nipples and glowing skin. Well, the damage was done. He'd seen all she had to offer, and he wasn't running away into the night. Awkward, she whispered, "Trace, I—"

"Shh," he murmured, trailing kisses down the side of her neck, pulling her arms around him more securely, backing her into the side wall of the shower.

The tile felt cold against her back, but she let him trap her there, enjoying every moment. As she tangled her fingers into his wet, silky hair, her body felt vibrant and pulsing, and her skin tingled with cool water and fiery caresses.

She was alive. She was happy. She was in love and in lust and everything else in between. Jubilant, Mabel beamed up at him, enjoying the power of these new feelings, of this one incredible moment in time. Tightening her arms around him, she widened her smile, trying to share all the joy and hope she felt lighting her up from the inside out.

But then she hesitated. She was on top of the world, and Trace looked like he was going to die.

"Mabel?" His gaze was fierce and intent. "You

look like somebody just gave you a puppy on Christmas morning.''

"I'm happy. Is there something wrong with that?"

"I just want us both clear on what's happening here," he said tersely. "We're going to make love. Now. Here. Unless one of us stops it right now, this is irrevocable, last chance, no turning back. I'm not stopping. Are you?"

She'd show him puppies on Christmas morning! Angry, aroused, she didn't answer, just nibbled his lips hungrily, closed her eyes, and rose up on her tiptoes to fit her body against his.

"No," he commanded, holding her back. "You have to look me in the eye and say it out loud. I have to know that this is what you want, too. Say it, Mabel. Do you want me? Do you want this?"

Water sluiced down on top of her head, but she didn't care. If this was the place, so be it. This was definitely the man.

She met his gaze defiantly. She might be dizzy and light-headed with desire, but she knew her own mind.

"I want you more than I've ever wanted anything in my whole life," she said huskily. "If you don't make love to me in the next three seconds, I'll go out of my mind."

"Done," he said darkly, "but it's going to take more than three seconds."

"Good." She grabbed his shirt and forced the finely spun fabric over his shoulders, slashing it out of the way.

"Great," he said roughly, tossing it aside.

"Perfect." Mabel ran her hands over the smooth, corded planes of his chest, filling her senses with the feel of him. Perfect? *Oh, yeah.* He felt wonderful. So slick, so hard, so male. She followed her hands with her mouth, licking rivulets of water away as they trickled over his warm, muscled skin.

He trembled under her mouth, and she felt drunk on her own power. Power. Over Trace. *Wow.*

But he bent to draw her back, one hand behind her head as he kissed her deep and fully. And that was the end of her power trip. Losing herself in the intoxicating, maddening sensations, she had to struggle to stay upright in the slippery tub.

Mabel was on fire. Little sparks flashed in the tips of her fingers, at the base of her spine, the slope of her shoulder, even her inner thigh, where it brushed his nubby trouser leg—anywhere he touched, anywhere he so much as glanced.

Her fingers shook as she reached for the top button of his pants. But Trace angled closer, keeping his insistent mouth on hers, clasping her hands, edging them back onto the tile, shoving them helplessly out of the way.

He was in charge of this sensual assault, holding her still, like a butterfly pinned to a board, to make it clear that he would set the pace. She could feel it, as his slow, agonizing rhythm reverberated through her body. It made her crazy, jittery, weak. Although they were both running on jagged nerves and frayed emotions, she already knew he was going to make her wait. And wait again.

He smiled, reckless and dangerous, his hips wedging her against the wall. She had no choice but to lock her legs around his waist to keep her balance. It felt incredible, slip-sliding along his hard body that way, letting the water splash between them, streaming in a direct line from the tips of her breasts to his washboard abdomen.

He dipped his head, intercepting the drops as they cascaded off her nipples. A moan of pure pleasure escaped her lips. Pleasure? Or water torture?

Torture. Absolute torture. A few seconds more, and she couldn't bear it.

Mabel twisted her hands away, winding them around his neck. She tilted his head back, brushing greedy little kisses over his cheeks and his forehead.

His lips and his hands slid over her, picking up the pace. As the flames between them stoked higher, hotter, she knew he was as turned-on, as out of control, as she was.

Beneath her, his fingers tugged at the top button of his pants, finally managing to shed them. As she could tell so very easily, the only thing under those was skin. The last bit of clothing between them had just dropped at his feet.

She had imagined him for so long, she would have liked to pull back and drink him in with her eyes, get her fill at last. But there was no time for that—not now. Feeling wild, wanton, Mabel tightened her legs around his hips, pressing as near as she could get, urging him to take that last leap.

"Now?" she whispered unsteadily, breathing the word into his ear.

He kissed her hard and quick. His arms held her so tightly, she couldn't catch her breath as he began to move underneath her, and she felt him so close.

"Yes," she murmured, bracing herself, anticipating his thrust.

Suddenly the water from the shower turned frigid, and the pressure of the spray doubled, blasting them up and down. She cried out in surprise, opening her eyes, just as Trace slipped inside.

The contrast of icy water and blazing, relentless man magnified her sensations. She shuddered with desire, clinging to him, clutching him, shattering around him way too hard and fast to take in.

But Trace stroked again and again, smooth and deep, and Mabel plunged into his rhythm, climbing again, toppling again, with mindless ease. She was already so aroused, she could only moan and hang on, gasping for air.

Trace arched into her, finding his own release hard upon the heels of hers. He held her for a moment, not moving, his head tipped to rest against hers, his heart beating steadily slower next to her breast.

Finally, as freezing water poured over them, Trace released her enough to slide her down his body, setting her back on her feet. He kissed her cheek and gazed into her eyes. There was a question there, and she hoped she knew the right answer.

His eyes were so blue, his lashes wet and thick. Filled with unexpected tenderness and awe, Mabel tried to recover some kind of poise. Or at least the ability to stand without collapsing like a wet noodle. She felt like crying. She felt like shouting with joy. She felt like clasping him to her and never letting go.

"Wow," she breathed after a moment, unable to think of anything else to express the inexpressible. *I love you* was flashing in her brain like a Times Square marquee, but she was much too afraid to share that with him. Not at this fragile, special moment. "Wow," she said again. "That was…amazing."

"Cold showers are supposed to keep you away

from this, not make it worse,'' he murmured, nipping at her earlobe with his teeth. ''Want to try again?''

She laughed into his shoulder, weak with after-glow. Trust him to skewer the tension without even trying. At least this time he hadn't come up with any rhymes about tables or stables.

Looking him in the eye, she asked, ''How about the bed this time?''

''I like the way you think,'' he whispered, switching off the defective shower and swinging her up into his arms.

And then Trace carried Mabel off to bed, before either of them had a chance to screw it up.

As EARLY-MORNING sunlight beamed into her eyes, Mabel groaned and raised a hand to ward it off. Her brain was foggy, but her body felt like it had been steamrollered, like the coyote in all those cartoons.

''What in the world did I do last night?'' she mumbled into her pillow. Without lifting her head, she rubbed the back of her hand against her forehead, and then idly ran it through her hair. What was wrong with her hair? It felt stiff and strange, like it was sticking out in all directions. ''Did I go to bed with it wet?''

Wet hair. Late shower. Late-shower guest.

And then it all came back to her, in living, breathing Technicolor. Could it be? She held herself very still. Slowly, she tilted her chin enough to hazard a glance over her shoulder, to the other side of the bed.

''Oh, God.'' She hadn't dreamed it. Trace was still there, peacefully snoozing, one arm dangling down to the floor.

Mabel bolted upright, snatching the sheet to cover herself. Like that wasn't locking the barn door after the horse had been stolen. Trace had already seen every inch of her body, and pressed his lips to most of them.

"Yeah, but it was dark then," she whispered. "In the bright light of day, things look very different."

Funny, *he* didn't look any different. Over there, hanging half-off the bed, Trace was as gorgeous as ever. His dark hair was rumpled, and his lashes lay black and lush against his cheek. In fact, he had a sweet, vulnerable aspect she never would have associated with him. But it sure was cute. It made her want to smooth his hair and stroke his cheek.

Okay, enough of that moony stuff. Mabel let her gaze venture a little lower. The sheet draped across him at the hip, leaving all of his chest and one long, lean leg exposed. *Fabulous.*

Mabel sighed. It wasn't fair for him to be so damn good-looking, especially when she knew what she must look like right now.

"You know, if he was who he's supposed to be, he wouldn't have spent the night," she grumbled. "It's not fair. He's supposed to be this big playboy, and everybody knows those guys get out of town before the break of dawn."

Not this one. Maybe he was just very, very tired.

"He deserves to be exhausted," she said out loud, casting her mind back to a few more of last night's details.

"Mmmph."

Mabel froze. But he wasn't awake, just shifting in his sleep.

Why was she so afraid for him to wake? Why

couldn't she face him? It wasn't that last night wasn't wonderful—it was *beyond* wonderful—it was that she was fresh out of disguises to fool him with. Okay, so last night it had been dark, and they'd been wet, and very caught up in the moment.

But what would he do when he woke up and spied the real Mabel, the one with the pale, bare face, hair that had dried every which way, and not even a scrap of lingerie or a little perfume to sweeten the picture?

There was just one thing to do. She eased over the edge of the bed as noiselessly as possible, planning to sneak into the bathroom to repair what she could. She actually had a foot on the floor when she felt him stir behind her.

Caught. She'd been in midescape, and now Trace was nuzzling her neck. It felt so terrific, Mabel wanted to burst into tears. She squashed her hands over her hair, hoping to flatten it before he got a good look.

"Okay, what's wrong?" he asked, propping himself up on one elbow. "Do you have a headache?"

"Why would you think I have a headache?" she demanded, trying to hide under a tiny corner of sheet.

"Because you have your hands pressed to your head?" he asked tentatively, clearly walking on eggshells.

"I guess you should know the bad news right now," she said, rolling over, baring her plain face and wacky hair to his eyes. "If it was the siren in the red dress you wanted, or even the Biker Chick, you're going to be very disappointed in the real deal."

Trace lay back, full out, and laughed really hard. This didn't endear him to Mabel any.

"I knew it," she muttered. "You think I'm a joke."

"Mabel…" His tone was reproving as he reached for her, kissing her right on the top of her wayward hair. "Have you forgotten I took your 'before' pictures? I know what you look like."

"Yes, but knowing, and then thinking I've improved, and then going back to ground zero—I mean, *past* ground zero—that's got to be a disappointment," she argued. "Besides, you're under no obligation to stick around this morning, so you don't have to be nice. We both know it was just a one-night thing, and so, okay, the night's over. No harm, no foul."

"Do I get a word in here somewhere?" Trace sat up against the headboard, regarding her with a sparkle in his eyes and more than a touch of humor. "Mabel, you didn't let me finish. I took your 'before' photos, and that's when I fell in love with you, before the hot-stuff makeover even started."

"Hold it." Mabel swallowed, trying to decide if she'd heard what she just thought she'd heard. "Did you say…" Her voice had a funny squeak in it. She scooted closer, still holding the sheet up to her chin. "Did you say you fell in love with me?"

"What the hell did you think I was doing here?"

"Well, I mean, no one ever said… I mean, I didn't think—"

Trace lifted a dark, elegant eyebrow. "Are you trying to tell me you actually bought all that crap about one-night stands you just spouted? I thought you were trying to be funny."

"Of course not! I was…" She persisted, even though she was beginning to understand these were tricky waters she was attempting to navigate. "I was giving you an out, in case you needed one."

"I can make my own outs, thank you very much." He arched an eyebrow. "Why, Mabel Ivey, I'm beginning to think you lured me over here just to take advantage of me. Here I tell you I'm in love with you, and the best you can do is tell me it was a one-night thing, no harm, no foul." He waited. "Well?"

"I didn't take advantage of you," she protested, biting her lip. "I wouldn't. I couldn't."

"I know you couldn't. Sleep with someone you didn't care a lot about, I mean." His lips curved into a smug, self-satisfied smile. "So I figure you love me, whether you're willing to tell me or not. After all, we both know that all the women I photograph fall in love with me."

"Only half," she corrected.

"So?" Trace nabbed her and rolled over on top of her before she had a chance to flee. Gazing down into her eyes, brushing a tiny kiss onto the tip of her nose, he asked, "Which half are you in?"

"Oh, come on." She couldn't resist when he was this close, when he was pushing her down into the bed with the sheer force of his personality. "You know how I feel about you."

"Say it, Mabel." His lips were a centimeter away, his voice barely a murmur.

"How could I not love you?" she inquired softly, arching up into his kiss. "You're perfect. It was never exactly a fair fight."

"Fair? You want fair?" Trace reached under the sheet and began to tickle her unmercifully, until she was giggling and squirming down there. "You make me fall for you, and then you start running around in leather and lingerie and garter belts. And you know I had no intention of starting anything.''

"It wasn't my fault,'' she managed, pushing his hands away. Mabel narrowed her eyes. "So you admit it—you did like me better all tarted up.''

"No, Mabel,'' he whispered. "I like you better this way. Naked, in my bed, drowsy, ready to play games all morning…''

His hands were starting to get out of control again, and Mabel squealed as she did her best to elude him.

"I'm serious about this, Trace. I really need to know the truth.'' She hoped she didn't look as wistful and woebegone as she felt. "We both know I'm not your type. You've met and been with the most beautiful women in the world. How can I compete?''

Trace relented, falling back onto his side of the bed. "Yes, obviously I've met a lot of beautiful women, Mabel, and I've photographed most of them. Stunning, perfect women. But you know what? Most of them are as dull as dishwater.''

"Sure.'' She didn't buy it. Not for a second.

He turned, and his gaze was frank, uncompromising. "Knowing you, I've discovered something— something about myself. Beauty is fine. It's great. But when I wake up in the morning, when I go out on the town, when I stay in at night, I just want to be with the one who makes me laugh.''

"Makes you laugh?'' Mabel echoed. *Wow. Great answer.* If she hadn't already been head over heels for this man, that would have tied it. "I know you probably think that I wanted you from the beginning because you're so darn handsome and sexy and—''

"Did I already ask you about doing PR for me?''

he interrupted, curling an arm around her and reeling her in.

"Let me say this. This is important. I'm not superficial, you know. I really think—" She smiled, her heart filling with the joy of this new love thing. "I really think I fell for you because you were funny. You and your dopey rhymes. I love that about you. Of course, the drop-dead looks don't hurt."

"We never did make love on the table," he noted dryly, tugging her sheet away an inch at a time.

"My table would never hold us," she warned, feeling decidedly chilly as the cover left her. As Trace's hand closed over her breast, she whispered, "I'm starting to get the idea my sense of humor isn't all you're going for, here."

He smiled wryly. "Well, you can always wear your slip backward…"

"It was a teddy."

"Or crash into me in the lobby at *Real Men.*"

"Crash into you? You crashed into me!" she protested hotly.

The sheet dipped below her waist, and she knew she was losing the ability to argue with him.

His words had become lazy, even if his hands kept getting busier and busier. "Is that the way you're going to put it when you write the article, Mabel?" Trace trailed a finger over her stomach, making her quiver. "Rewrite a little history and make me the bad guy?"

"I don't know what I'm going to write yet," she said huskily. "Does it matter?"

"Mabel," he teased, "that doesn't sound like you. I thought this job meant everything to you."

It was hard to care when he was wearing less than

she was, when his thigh was nudging her hip, when his lips hovered near her breast, not quite touching, just daring her. Who cared about some stupid job at *Real Men?*

"Oh, no!" she said suddenly, sitting up, almost clonking him with her knee. "The job!"

"Mabel, I was kidding." He tried to soothe her with his hands, but she was off and running with a whole new case of panic.

"But what am I going to do?" she cried. "How can I write it now, after what's happened between us? To tell the whole story, I'm going to have to put in really personal stuff. I can't do that!"

Trace stopped her with a kiss, covering her mouth so she couldn't talk.

"Mmmph, rrrmph," she managed, until he backed off and she could make sense again. "I've also realized that this thing between us blows the whole thesis of the makeover issue. I mean, if you really did start to fall for me when I was still firmly in the 'before' category, then what good did it do me to try long nails and garter belts and thigh-high boots? You like the plain version!"

"I don't think you have a problem," he told her gently. "Go ahead—tell the truth. You had fun with your sexy makeover, you saw yourself in a new light, and you drove me crazy. So what if I'm in love with the authentic, unvarnished Mabel? We can always pull out the leather boots and the fishnets every now and again, can't we, just for fun?"

He looked so hopeful, Mabel couldn't help it. She had to laugh.

And wasn't that what made the two of them so

right for each other? Smiling, she vaulted over on top of him for a change.

"The boots, definitely. The fishnets—you've got to be kidding."

"I loved those fishnets," he objected.

"Okay, okay, throw in the fishnets, too." She tipped down to kiss his delicious lips. "You know, Trace, as long as we keep laughing, I think this is the beginning of a long and very hot relationship."

"Good."

"Great."

He smiled, and he was so adorable it took her breath away. "Perfect," he whispered. "Absolutely perfect."

Look for a new and exciting series from Harlequin!

HARLEQUIN

Duets ™

Two __new__ full-length novels in one book, from some of your favorite authors!

Starting in May, each month we'll be bringing you two new books, each book containing two brand-new stories about the lighter side of love! Double the pleasure, double the romance, for less than the cost of two regular romance titles!

Look for these two new Harlequin Duets™ titles in May 1999:

Book 1:
WITH A STETSON AND A SMILE
by Vicki Lewis Thompson
THE BRIDESMAID'S BET
by Christie Ridgway

Book 2:
KIDNAPPED? by Jacqueline Diamond
I GOT YOU, BABE by Bonnie Tucker

**2 GREAT
STORIES BY
2 GREAT
AUTHORS
FOR 1 LOW
PRICE!**

Don't miss it! Available May 1999 at your favorite retail outlet.

HARLEQUIN®
Makes any time special.™

Look us up on-line at: http://www.romance.net   HDGENR

Sultry, sensual and ruthless...

THE AUSTRALIANS

Stories of romance Australian-style, guaranteed to
fulfill that sense of adventure!

This April 1999 look for
Wildcat Wife
by Lindsay Armstrong

As an interior designer, Saffron Shaw was the hottest ticket
in Queensland. She could pick and choose her clients, and
thought nothing of turning down a commission from Fraser
Ross. But Fraser wanted much more from the sultry artist
than a new look for his home....

*The Wonder from Down Under: where spirited women win
the hearts of Australia's most independent men!*

Available April 1999
at your favorite retail outlet.

HARLEQUIN®
Makes any time special ™

LOOK FOR OUR FOUR FABULOUS MEN!

Each month some of today's bestselling authors bring
four new fabulous men to Harlequin American Romance.
Whether they're rebel ranchers, millionaire power brokers
or sexy single dads, they're all gallant princes—and
they're all ready to sweep you into lighthearted fantasies
and contemporary fairy tales where anything is possible
and where all your dreams come true!

You don't even have to make a wish…
Harlequin American Romance will grant your every desire!

Look for Harlequin American Romance
wherever Harlequin books are sold!

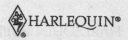

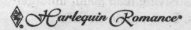

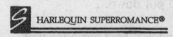